Through the shades

"Nothing is"

Nothing is as important as it seems.

What seems important is actually, nothing!

Month of March, Goa!

<u>Acknowledgements:</u>

To Goa- the journey from Airport to the Candolim beach.

To the hospitality industry for providing papers and pencils for writers everywhere

To Garima - who as a matter of fact expressed "Why don't you write?" when I asked how her book was coming along.

To Husband dear

To Benny Kurian

To my brothers

To YOU

CHAPTER 1

Present

"Ma'am it is called moon roof in this part of the world" the car salesperson remarked, as Ria checked out the machine on wheels. "Ahhh I see...." retaliated Ria, returning his smile and thoroughly beaming within, for it had been after all a reinforcement of the quick decision being right. The decision to migrate to sun drenched Sharjah, from the sun-deprived, chirpiness deprived, chaos deprived, almost life deprived London. Even when the house there met the promises of being centrally heated, hardwood floored and part automated. Along with paid electricity, lady assistant for chores twice a week, commute and so much more provided, in central London.

Just after the arrival at the Emirates lounge a few days back, the ease of March air through the vents of a huge air-conditioning system had a cool, soothing effect on her skin. It was nothing like the taciturn and cold Heathrow. She had to rush to the restroom in order to shed the layers of warm inner linings.

The signage on the escalators instead of "Mind the Gap" read "Mind the Abaya"- whatever that meant.

The glitz and opulence all around was imperious, almost overbearing. One could easily forget the business of exiting the airport and venturing into the city, having been enormously distracted inside. A consumer paradise! She picked a few knick-knacks, including Sumit's favourite drink and glided around the elaborate merchandise spread. Suddenly she regained the sense of time through a crystal Swarovski watch looking out at her through a flawless engineered stone framed and extra clear glass show window. Crossing several other visual distractions amidst the clear signage, she rushed towards the exit.

Gucci glasses, moccasins, chic shirt! Was he the same 'brand unconscious' husband of hers? He looked rather ritzy. She ran to hug him. The time lost in waiting didn't seem to have bothered him. He seemed casual and stayed put. His response to her hug was rather awkward." What's wrong?" whooped out automatically from her lips, although she had fondled with many other opening lines en-route.

" Nothing" he said and here was the sweet smile she had so dearly missed, the properly measured elongation of the lips, which could melt hearts in a twinkling, the most malleable heart being her own. She again brought up arms around his neck, trying to deliver the exact scene replaying in her dreamy head, in her seven hours of journey. Again, his response was cold. She was taken aback by the coldness of her soul mate. "Ria Jaan, this is a conservative country." Oh, that made it simple, a relief! It was about the country they were in and not anything between them.

Huddled amongst Dubai's duty-free bags in the four-wheel drive, she tried to absorb if she was in a war-laden kind of a country because of his shushing her down as she brought up the subject of a novel, recently read about closer geographies to UAE. She was trying to orient herself through questions brimming in her head. But now she tried to distract herself from the conversation. Well, the surroundings looked shipshape and well laden, the avenues wide and the profusion of roadside flowers in Dubai made a pretty sight at spring's behest. The crispness of the side-veiled Ethiopian lady driver and her command on the wheel, decent abiding of systems left her impressed. But the steering was on the wrong side, cars were zooming past from the wrong lane or maybe she was in the wrong country in the desert. Desert, but where was the desert?

There were layers of vegetation. Beautiful flowers in the forefront, shrubs and then palm trees, followed by interestingly shaped buildings. The avenues stretched wide and fantastic machines drove past. The equidistant palm trees, neatly lined turf and the colourful profusion of flowers at the edges of the roads framed the avenues neatly.

One flower centre, a striking built form of bays, resembling huge splayed petals specially entrapped her. And also striking were the neat lines of cladding on the elevation of the police station building. Later this building was to be the initiation point of a comparative study with the police station and the state of affairs back home, between Sumit in conversation with anybody and everybody.

The architecture was modern mostly, and some buildings were pretty impressive. Where was downtown Dubai? The mail sent to her by a friend had shown rapid development on lines of postmodernism and high-tech architecture. And she remembered being fascinated by the challenging construction of Burj-Al-Arab in the water! Especially the huge mast façade as watched on Discovery. Now she wanted to see it herself.

Her reverie was soon broken. Was it the sun or the Urdu the lady seated ahead spoke, the fresh breeze outside swaying the blooms, the proximity of this place to Delhi or something else? She felt "at home" in the very first hour in the country.

Out came her camera and with a change of lens went zoom, hands steadied, ISO checked, aperture set, breath controlled and she captured the motion blur. And soon the fantastic cars froze in the movement against the blurred background. The gigantic bonnets of a Cadillac Escalade, the classiness of an Alfa Romeo, sleekness and speed of a fresh yellow Lamborghini, fierceness of a Ford Mustang, Shelby cobra, menacing look of Dodge charger SRT........ Was it Bugatti with a side skirt in striking colour with the vents? It was getting challenging to keep a tab of the amazing machines and the difficult names.

In order to absorb as much as possible of the surroundings, she missed the transition from Dubai to Sharjah, if there was any formal one. Now the mounds bore flowerbeds blooming in formation to read 'Welcome to Sharjah' by the roadside. The perpendicular road to the mounds, she was told, had been a runway in times of the Sharjah matches. Now it was called King Faisal road. Sumit now looked approachable and they started an exchange of notes. The camera went back into the covers.

The vehicle turned into a street, lined with villas, pavements and some foliage. The side veiled Egyptian lady driver took a perfect U-turn from the rightmost lane, cut out of the wide divider for the very purpose of facilitating U-turns, without hampering the speed of the vehicles zooming straight by. The neighbourhood was phenomenally neat and quiet and the duo set towards their new nest.

The villa was an enchanting one. It was the year 2006, mobiles generally were not smart yet, people were. Everything about oneself and the rest didn't travel around in a flash through mobiles. People still bought and used maps in hard copies. In their conversation on landlines and Sumit's Sony mobile, she hadn't had an inkling of the place, the villa and the surroundings. And there were so many issues to be catered to before the move. All she could make out from the conversations in the last fortnight was that he had been safe here and busy replacing the yellow light fixtures in the house with fluorescent ones. About his setting up the house entirely, any information about the country or any such detail, she hadn't the faintest idea.

The porch- less main entrance opened to the entrance foyer of the villa. Plenty of sunshine reflecting off the surfaces, pretty much-uncovered floor between immaculately placed furniture added up to the sheer volume of space as the first impression. The air conditioning in the entire house was pre-set at an easy temperature. The rooms and the kitchen, the washrooms - all felt comfortable at a similar coolness. It was an orderly property, not ornate with high false ceilings and without the marring of fans.

Entering through the foyer was the right order, unlike walking directly into the living room as in her childhood house in Vasant Kunj, New Delhi. Entering the Delhi home always felt like barging into a private space. She went around the whole villa like a curious child. There were table covers done in vintage pattern besides the rest and tissue paper boxes placed in all the rooms.

Sumit seemed to have taken so much care in placing them aligned to the edges of tables. It didn't go unnoticed by her and was evident in her smile. The portion of the villa allocated to him by his company was perfect for the two of them and she rushed to see the two bedrooms on the first floor. Lo, behold! In the balcony from the master bedroom, the view was of wonder. In the distance was the sea. The Sea! Sumit was now beaming and relishing her reaction. An astounded her, made all of it worth his effort.

The two of them stood outside, just looking afar for a while. She was apprehensive about going ahead and touching him and waited until he held her, once inside. "Didn't you miss me" she wanted to hear about his longing.

"O, you are my breath…..And I didn't miss breathing at all" and they surrendered into each other's arms. That was liberating and connecting too.

'Wind beneath my wings' was playing in her mind.

Love is flight itself!

Being in love and in harmonious sharing of lives is an alluringly natural feeling, like breathing, which makes you ponder, how were your breaths accounted for before.

Ambling by the night was on the uncluttered pavements. There were no cyclist paths and tactile paving like in the UK and the triangular edging of transition strips between pavement and road were missing. So were the pelican crossings. On the right side of Corniche Road was a huge dockyard, with ships of all sizes stalled. The huge blue ones stood out and were of the local police. Wooden boats were also anchored, adding a rustic charm to the overall plethora.

Night began to deepen only on the watch but not in the general atmosphere. She noticed a large number of boxes, big and small, merchandise labelled of all kinds in the dockyard. Smaller packets were overflowing. They looked like cakes of soap and other toiletries out of wooden cartons. Gradually the people receded. She looked around for security and there was none. It felt abnormal. Soon the place was abandoned. It was kind of exciting now; almost an urge to try out flicking intended to tease the security system.

They walked towards the market. Orderly shops, however small or big, had an air conditioner hanging out and no CCTV. It was getting too late but the vibe was adventurous, so they hung for a little while more.

The basis of this was the trust in harsh laws and fear of them, Sumit explained. That was difficult to digest, hailing from North India. Again, she had the urge to pickpocket a little and walk home.

She stepped out of the house on her own, the third day. Sumit had instructed her to check both directions before crossing the road and to strictly use pedestrian crossing. It would take a few days to get accustomed, he had added. Off she went, walking a long distance before she stepped down on the narrow slip road from under the flyover. She then stopped for the zooming white four-wheeler to pass. The white kaffeyah and kandura clad Arab in the vehicle halted and waited. Had she committed any mistake, was her first thought. Finally, he signalled with his hand to cross. Back home you would cross the road so differently, waiting for the cars to pass by and not vice-versa. Pedestrians did have a right of way here.

But then crossing a roundabout was tedious. One couldn't barge into the roundabout in order to reach the opposite diagonal. You did have to cross four roads for that. After a few days, she did try crossing it by Delhi's principal of walking minimum distance, screeched and halted a lot of traffic and learnt her lesson. The roundabouts were free of traffic lights and were always with a loop of moving vehicles. Before a vehicle entered a roundabout, the driver had to ascertain that no other vehicle was entering from his left and then could zoom into the roundabout, without hoping for a newly arrived young Indian lady making her way through a short- cut.

People lived in Sharjah and worked in Dubai, she recollected; and they crossed a nightmarish traffic route. Sumit's office was in Sharjah itself. As it turned out later, she liked the character of Sharjah more than that of Dubai's. She could better relate to this emirate even though Dubai's atmosphere was much more cosmopolite and thrilling. It was perfect for weekends.

CHAPTER 2

The SEA!

Most astounding of the change in her routine was the vicinity of the sea. Of the seascape as an integral part of daily living! Never had she an inkling of following the pattern of waves over the stretch of the day. Having been on beaches occasionally on a holiday away from landlocked Delhi, now gripped by the ocean was unusual, yet very strong an affinity. She was thankful for the limited and brief early ocean encounters; this one had the newness of an experience beyond comparison, joy of a new untainted friendship. The sea had kind of a routine of its own, albeit changed the patterns often, just like her. In this instant friendship, with the beach as rendezvous, was forming an everyday experience in the realms of serendipity.

Added to this effect was attar, from the oudh lit outside the bedroom in the morning. A new aroma and looking ahead to an encompassing, promising day! The Al-fisht beach across the Corniche provided enough shots of the motion trails and sometimes of people for street photography. Photographing from the pavement, her feet were pulled towards the cool, salty receding water and the soothingly refreshing light beige sand in between. The picturesque beach was practically vacant most of the time in the working hours but for an occasional lady in a burqa or a bystander in white Kandura. The only regular visitor was the machine in the noon, whirring and immaculately cleaning the sand.

Around two hundred feet stretch of it in width; the sand was of lightest pink, beige and subsequently cream shades towards the water. Each of the seven emirates that the country comprises of, had a different colour of sand, as said. Towards the roadside, there were a few podiums with semi-circular concrete seats around a post supporting a wide thatched umbrella. Advancing towards the waves, absorbing the whole scene in day by day, the expanse of the sands, the water ahead, the sky, her own lightness and feeling of spring in the feet, she would reach a point where the Corniche traffic noise ceased to reach the ear. The mind involuntarily switched off the world and feet sunk in the light hue sand. Now the waves would start singing softly. This was her favourite moment when the thrilled feet picked up speed and the upthrust reduced. She would drop her camera bag at this juncture and transcend further, carrying herself alone with vigour, as if the camera hurdled or just didn't fit in this frame. Exhilarated, she could almost run to embrace the clean, cold water.

Wasn't the sea's response of welcoming her feet, washing away the sand just under their impression, worth every penny of not thinking about any other job in the world and giving herself in to this beloved?

The three ships at international boundaries in the distance became anchor points for the eyes. Many a times they became the subject of her pictures, just like the umbrellas against a backdrop of sandy, light smoothened particles. Her lunch and book too started accompanying soon, the hours whiled away in immersed serendipity. A series on the images of translucent waves in proximity in different lighting conditions, ships and skies, lives around them came out in prints, well documented for further use.

When all you want to do in love is just to feel being in love!

The walking exploration started gaining distance from home in a matter of days. The mosque nearby was on the same side as the sea. It was on the Corniche after Radisson. It had a Mashrabiya covering the tower's façade. But the built form sheltered and encompassed it with an irregular elevation. The Mashrabiya stood upright, like a saving grace in the day and mesmerising by evening. Light exuded out of its geometric patterns in exuberance! The sciography produced by the built forms in relationship to each other and the quality of illumination created an aura of awe in a unified way. The optical patterns on the paving and on the turf harmonized in an enchanting manner.

She lowered the camera on the stand in order to capture the play of the same on the turf, paving and on the feet of worshipers walking towards the mosque. On the perpendicular plane, the top of her frame covered by various shaped bokeh. In her pictures, the highlights in the shadows of mashrabiya's intricate pattern would require working. She wasn't keen on sitting in front of the laptop yet, but what had to be done had to be done.

Such interesting elements and more in the play of artificial light and the evening setting by beheld her. The evening light was aplenty but when the lights in the towers were switched on, it was as if to welcome the evening and to proclaim our dependence on that artificial means for vision. It was rightly called the golden hour. The effect would be the unequalled beauty of the jali work, the edges of each opening chiselling out the pattern glowing in the warm yellow light. Also, the reminiscent effect of the setting sun!

And with the pavement signifying the narrow balance our lives oscillated between -ever running after material dreams and nature's way.

The offsetting spaces between the road and the built block had multi-levels of landscaping, mostly hard and ornately detailed wrought iron lampposts. So were the benches, equally detailed with golden highlights all along the shore with very few people sitting.

She would notice and pick shells on the beach sometimes. Many shells looked like rosebuds. Later she discovered, only in the month of March did her pal, the sea, churn out the rose-shaped ones, spiralling whites in marble. What a welcome was that for spring from a pristine beach!

March gave way to April and so did the pleasant weather to not-so-pleasant one and further on to absolutely uncomfortable. Having had to walk in the unbearable heat by April's end and cross four roads in order to reach the nearest pharmacy, which wasn't at a motorable distance and halting of a taxi on the Corniche being a stroke of luck, she decided to own a car. Lots of stories circulated about the cruel Kachcha and Pakka test and of the kind of money and effort spent in the process. She was undeterred; the walk for the medicine had given her the clarity for the next step. She enrolled herself to learn driving.

The Kachcha test involved some written classes initially. This country had some facilities in disguise for the protected gender, one of them being skipping the classes for the written test. The driving instructor in the yellow Nissan Sunny was Zahra, of Pakistani origin and clad in a burqa. She was a proficient driver but talkative to the highest degree. On the drive, her stories involved her five children and a husband working in the state-run used-car evaluation facility.

This well-versed female, if Ria had met otherwise, she wouldn't in her extended imagination, associate with her knowledge of cars. The non-stop chatterbox and hell of an instructor was soon to leave for a two-month vacation to Pakistan. Paramount was her concern about carrying water, a certain gallon per person, the total being seven of them, multiplied by the days in a long vacation was the highlight of her banter of the day. It was to this end that, with the visual of water gallons in her head, Ria drove as per the instructions imparted by the teacher.

Zahra had instructed little and let the student flow on her own and stressed on details like the apt holding of the steering, use of back and side mirrors, physical checks, strict up keeping with the traffic rules and checking all signage. She was happy with the apprentice's driving and asked for an assurance that further classes would be taken diligently after the Kachcha and waived off the last few classes. Ria assured her the same and bid her well. The yellow Nissan sunny dropped Ria home after clearing the Kachcha test, which she had passed with an "excellent" for her reverse parallel parking skills as taught. Zahra was exultant too and as usual, her set of steering and the controls of the car were unused, her full focus on the recital of water gallons having been packed, as she dropped Ria home, a fine audience to her talkative self. Another day Zahra took her on an unusual route and Ria returned with another vantage point for her shoot identified. She would return with her gear.

Ria called up Sumit in his office from the landline, bluffing. After he spent a long cool- her- down conversational effort, for none of his colleagues had made it in the first go and in fact, Zafar had spent almost two-three years before obtaining one, Tarun a year because he had chosen manual instead of automatic and so on. She couldn't stand the excitement anymore and blurted out about a few classes waived off by Zahra and having passed in flying colours. The tenor from the other side made her day.

CHAPTER 3

Two years back

Amidst all the commotion in the house, father pointed out the hunk on the bike to her from the balcony, at their Vasant Kunj house in New Delhi. She was dressed in yellow ethnics for the puja, the entire day of which mother had imposed at home. The tiny, very beautiful idols of Gods in crystals and a few in bronze at the altar were also dressed in yellow and white silks, finely beaded in gold and silver on the edges. The revving up of those engines was enough to create a sensation, without a look at the jacket and helmet-clad hunk. The tasks at hand thrown aside, she alighted the flight of stairs in alacrity, the beaded bronze dupatta sweeping the treads behind swiftly. The biker seemed a little taken aback by the elaborate attire of his prospective pillion rider. Did her excitement even leave him with a possibility to contemplate and remark or to pay salutations to anyone else standing in the balcony? She quickly plopped herself onto the bike and keeping up with the momentum of the entire scene, Sumit sped. The amazement, the closeness on the wheels, the cold polluted air against the closed eyes felt like thrilled meditation. A few minutes of riding on Sumit's scrambler bike before he left for his work, revved her own engines too. The dreary religious rites ahead went through easily.

Everything portrayed itself in the form of a story usually, as a fresh story unfolds at dawn. Out to enjoy the magic of the early hours, she slowed her pace in the neighbouring street where the long green swaying twigs and the tiny leaflets touched her head and continued the conversation they were having. Or was it that she could speak passably with herself in that lane lined with Gulmohar, smoothly flourishing on one side along the road. Tin screens by the roadside kept the empty plots and the garbage hidden from view.

Lightning and thunder in the background highlighted in flashes the tiny glinting droplets as translucent adornments on the tiny leaves. Also, the edges of red flowers lightening up in colour provided a watery gradation, otherwise non-visible in the day.

In times like these, one could feel the rhythm in the walk. Or maybe the walk overtook and became symphonic with her! The lack of pruning had supplemented and added a lovely touch, the leaves brushing against your head and opening a dialogue. Their scale sensed the relation to humans. And the long horizontal leaves with tiny leaves in an array, if an artist were to sketch, would be mesmerizing in charcoal. The wind was getting rid of the weaker yellow ones, fashioning their fall in a silent rain.

Serenity! She loved to be with herself at such a time; a subtle smile formed on her lips and the same reflected in her gait.

A slightly overcast day captured the shadows and mood of the morning well. The sciography, as a muted accessory to the frames, heightened the sense of depth. And the subjects, as in a hide and seek game, play around the light with the scenes, the people, the buildings. One of the images was worth locking in, the essence of the foreground captured in kids splashing in the potholes in the background. As it started to pour, she dashed towards home.

Rain, the most non-committal entity, changed direction and speed of the fall at a whim! It played with the luminescence and rendition of the awaiting sun, not letting it in for the entire stretch of the day.

It chose one section of the wooden bench, embedded in the balcony railing, to dance in a continuous fall, accompanied by its pitter-patter sound. The rhythm built up, as in the notes of music, and one could dance. Once its announcing entry was done with, it rained quietly and smoothly for long. The beautiful consistent sort now, the parent clouds not in any kind of rush. The trees enjoying the stillness and then with the wind breaking into a charming movement with bunches of flowers as the centre stage. The leaves on the edges trying some frantic dancing!

Now was one of the best times to shoot, post the downpour. Camera had become an extension of hers.

She had started noticing the balance between mass and void in the buildings, the behaviour of spaces in a different light, the effect of surroundings, biorhythm, and the moods of people in general.

The built form in some buildings with their strong geometry seemed like a frozen concerto now. The play of light and shade imparted texture and depth to the artistic renderings of the frames. And they increasingly got noticed as she grew interested in the subject of interplay, travelled, and exposed herself to varied structures. The old forts had mischievous stories to tell and many to hide; the modern buildings were more blatant and direct. Some of the builder housings lacked persona. Rural structures had a very lived-in characteristic. Empathy, serenity, sometimes hypocrisy, spoke in high volumes in different spaces.

The sun is resting

No hush no rush

Not even your own sound

Lo! Behold this!

But I still wonder

What if my viewfinder was round!!

On one wall of her bedroom, opposite the bay window seating, hung the print of a portrait by photographer Jay Maisel, brought as a gift by a distant uncle from the United States. It was a tight frame and spoke volumes. On a clear background, the soft skin tone of the girl got a profuse contrast from the red sheet with a sheen that she was lying on. The striking play of light and shade which left you gaping, indeed was, in essence, a painting with light, something she had read about photography in the book and on the few lessons she had on a CD.

The relaxed body form on the folded fabric texture suggested that she had rolled onto the bed, daydreaming. The expression of the girl spoke not only of stories untold but of the future too. Youthful, hopeful dreams, yet to be realized. Dream and the dreamer frozen in a frame! The photographer had put his subject at an evocative ease, enough so to let her think and be in her space. He himself seemed unobtrusive, in the space, allowing her to be in her element. Angular form of the body imparted to the portrait an abundance of dynamism.

Ria always imagined this picture to be hung in the subject's room too and would be inspiring her, connecting her to hope, art and beauty of life and most importantly- the power to grip belief. Belief! The photographer had let the option open for the viewer to imagine and complete the body form in imagination. This effect would have been lost, in case the whole arm or face was taken in the frame. It was a personification of the might of gesture. A manifesto of what she read, "I don't see light as something that falls, it seeps in and scatters as natural as the texture of the surface is."

Earlier she had Robert Doisneau's framed picture of the kiss in Paris, another of the prints Uncle had got. She was in awe of Paris's Street and the captured moment of a kiss suspended in the air. Only one day when she stumbled about it in a book, of how the image was staged by actors with the photographer walking behind, did she bring it down from her wall, packed and stacked. It kind of felt like being cheated.

Now this young girl with untold dreams and the reckless hope which naïves of the world are hugely bestowed with, was synonymous to herself. She didn't know what, but metaphorically something good was about to happen, around the corner. Always!

She took her portfolio of pictures of the buildings and street photography to the prospective employers, from the list jotted down from the Internet. The portfolio also contained a series on seasons; the strongest segment was of rains in Delhi. The falling of the drops practically translated into the resonance of mood, through the camera.

"Call me on Monday," said the polite, occupied looking young architect. That look, she gathered later, was inbuilt in the young guy's trait- solving innumerable aspects of the design, wondering how to tally it with the finances and building services and so on. She landed up in his office and he graciously employed her on an assignment of documenting the progress of a temple belonging to his sect on the Karnal highway to begin with. His was a single room set up, a studio cum office in Defence Colony.

Morning in the office started with a cleaning guy coming over and the architect having to complain about his punctuality. This didn't really go well with the idea of an office; the boss having had to scold the cleaning guy. It was more of a ritual reserved for her house patented by her mom or maybe by all the moms in the country. Well, clearly the ritual extended to the crisp looking professionals too, here.

Onto her first assignment as the boss instructed firmly before she gathered her wits, she was jotting out minutes of meeting from his last day's consultation. Though she started as an alien to the concept of minutes of meeting, she fought a compelling urge to refuse a secretarial task. And she, a person who loved the dictatorship of a small nib on a white paper, started enjoying the jargon associated with architecture, the knick-knacks of the project, the structures, the discussion about proportions and the role and value of the stakeholders soon.

Her formation of letters on paper was admired by the architect but the minutes of meeting could not be scanned and faxed across. So, she had to type and mail them across.

Accompanying him next, to a discussion of the on-going project for jotting down minutes of meeting, she tried to acclimatize herself furthermore on the understanding of this trade. These discussions would repeatedly move towards an argument of the sort but subsided in the realm of professionalism. The other day the architect was explaining the juxtaposition of masses in tandem, the well-travelled client was pointing out at the elevations and quoting examples from his recent trip to Angkor Wat. It seemed to be a tussle between mathematics and philosophy of design. The client was sharing a mathematical sum, the structural designer trying to solve it.

The architect was trying to explain the spaces evolving sequentially, starting from a concept document called "design brief". He was kind of getting there in his narrative, if only allowed to speak without interruption. His narrative was of luxurious spaces flowing into the next set, almost intuitively. Of fleeting and changing sciography on the wall and winter sun executing artistic expression on the facades!

He had spoken of interconnectivity amongst spaces, jotted by her and now pinned as bullet points on the board. She was reading and visualizing when the music he played broke her musing. She was musing about the images of the succulent earth colour, enriched by the winter sun and comprehending details of gradual layering of mass on the Shikhara of one block. And they both set into working for the rest of the day.

Next day a vendor visited without appointment while the boss was on site. After having compiled the information required for her next day's shoot, she was browsing through piles of magazines. An article she came across in an old copy of Times of India about the recollection of Kargil war, the images moved her so and she snivelled. She wiped her tears at the ring of the bell and attended to the vendor who must have left a sample booklet in the huge stash earlier. For the first time it occurred to her that it could be unsafe being locked in with strangers and decided to address it. The boss came back in the afternoon and busied himself on the phone. His random glance noticing her bulges of bust while being in conversation on phone made her uncomfortable as sharpening of one's sixth sense does, in that matter. And there was nothing more to discuss.

Next, she joined as a trainee, under her father's recommendation, the studio of photographer Abhiyansh, who was earlier a photojournalist. Now he undertook all kinds of assignments and taught young photographers. He was quite reputed for working within an ethical framework as gathered by her dad.

Abhiyansh was a tall, well-built guy. Sharp looks, ears pierced, dressed smartly in full sleeve shirt, jeans, and boots. He was enormously respectful of war photographers who gave opportunity to the world of getting to know the reality- people to people connection. It was hard on him, trying to reintegrate once he moved from war journalism. Of been there, seen the trauma, anguish, and suffering! Those people could have been somebody's entire world.

He got sick of not knowing which side to write for, the side which was dying or the one killing out of duty and of wondering if he would regret it later in his life, in retrospect. Getting the pictures cleared for publishing, dealing with the endless mar sometimes was an ordeal. And then there was accusation of mala fide intention from the bureaucratic lobby. He had closed himself on the topic and distanced himself from the bureaucratic lobby altogether.

Now he would talk of generosity and courage and valour of humans in lectures at universities, more than the effect of atrocities. But his mind would sometimes go numb with the memories. Photography is a solo profession he said- you have to be in touch with your own feelings. The ground realities of war demanded Introspection and awareness at the same time. Also the value of love, compassion and of living!

"Don't let the bad have the best of you", he said to the young minds. How the war photojournalists chased their own wild side and pursued the endearing end of resolving political differences and enhancing the sensible nous of humanity. The shots of ferociousness, dearth, guns at ease in hands and madness in the eyes, silence between the shootouts, human cries of shock and wounds in the sacks being carried by equally wounded legs. He could think of "them" endlessly.

Journalism demanded respect. The same stood true for reporters and writers in general. He gave the example of responsible writers. They too had an ethical responsibility of a tolerant view of the lives of the needy and desperate, "the rogue and the tricksters", he remembered, as quoted by a writer.

He had recalibrated himself but not forgone humanitarian crisis. Rather he started picking up soft voices now, voices otherwise hushed or living in dissent. In one of his recently published series, he captured faces of women in various locations of the world, unheard of countries too, just the faces-straight on, eyes open or closed, grinning or frowning or blank or deceptive or serene. Women in veils and face paints and ones in all allure! They were the fragments of the world, like the gripping parts of geography and also of varied poetry. Those images held onto you.

A journey of exploration and the find!

Find was the key element. Another series he did on hands, of all kinds of men and how much they spoke of affection, labour, need and deceit.

The legal issues in the practice, he also taught his students, were to be avoided at all costs possible. Nothing broke the spirit of an artist's establishment more than being on the other side of the law. And his establishment had a zero tolerance for plagiarism.

Ria was hired as an apprentice for a period of six months. She, with a team, was sent as an observer to a conference in a high-end hotel. Her work didn't impress Negi Kishore. Next, she was sent to cover a closed group discussion about financial attraction for investors along with a senior photographer. Each had to operate individually though.

The venue was in a five-star property like her last assignment. The ceilings of this hotel were neater, straight lined. In the conference room no giant, turtle sized chandeliers bulged out of the ceilings, few lights instead, which were efficient - simply emitting light as they should, colours of the room muted in order to aid focused conversations. The people seemed to be thought leaders for others outside the room to follow. The talk was about the quality of disclosure in India being nowhere close to what investors were looking for, investor risk not understood and how disclosure could lead to better investments.

During the introduction break, Ria approached Parika, who was furiously gazing into her laptop. She spoke briefly about herself and returned to her screen, politely excusing herself on the pretext that she was to be asked a question next from the director of global infrastructure and added that it was to be about risk management and the opportunity lens.

Oh! All these meetings had a pre-set introduction and pre-set closure, she observed. Also, the presentations were mostly run incomplete, proceedings hard pressed with time. Parika spoke about the risk becoming a compliance measure, how data heaped, being a repository of reports, how they could guide companies to attract the right investors, how to overcome credit worthiness and how to match make with the right investors. Disclosure, she said, was the middle name.

She took pictures of Parika, the Sardar guy who had approached her, the German who was the moderator, the messy-haired lady in the rust orange jacket, the gentleman in the olive shirt and jute jacket, one of the two asking random but relevant questions. He spoke about practical integration of writing a project duly, to develop it and about resources and capacity building. His question was elaborate and directed to everyone. Relevant, but not pre doctored, nobody seemed prepared or willing to answer. Well, the conference had to be propelled on. The reluctant director started speaking by saying he would briefly answer and actually uttered the briefest possible answer in a complicated jargon. The gentleman in the olive shirt lost his enthusiasm for a discussion, which he had displayed while initiating. The discussion moved to errant taxation leading to projects being non feasible.

She took some candid shots of the director, of the young man blinking his eyes at the young lady sitting opposite in an acknowledgement to her smile as she looked up from her notes. She looked up from her notes when white haired Mr Bagai spoke about the real scenario, how he frankly didn't know what he had achieved in his six years tenure going back and forth, how the trees were supposed to be planted for Delhi metro project, how because of the lack of land, fine had to be submitted instead and done with. Accordingly, how the trees were cut in lieu of monetary fine, how he was troubled about things actually not happening but being portrayed as investor enthusiasm.

He remarked in between - "We are so busy in performance reviews that we forget to perform". That was the statement that made Ria stop and capture an exasperated image of this man. His words moved the discussion to a reality bit. The moderator cut him down on the pretext of exceeding time. Mr Bagai did stop with a bang of pencil on the paper. The moderator closed the session smilingly, adding that he would put some optimism back into the discussion. This was met by a knowing smile from the gentleman in the olive shirt and his smile was met by the lady in an orange jacket and hers by the person across the table watching her.

The summary was simple - however big the profile of a discussion, the most straight and logical points impacted the most.

The frank photographs of the participant's expressions again met with Naag's displeasure. Where were the formal images of an event of similar decorum in her set of results? He did take note of the full frame image she had shot of the venue while people were being seated at the beginning of the session. She had observed that on a rectangular table, the heads had to be craned in order to see the presentation on the wall and the table with curved edges worked better. She had jotted that too under the photograph. This time she was duly sent to meet Abhiyansh in order to be relieved of the office.

Inside Abhiyansh's large cabin lay the fish eye lens she had been eyeing since very long, lying idly at the white desk just in front of her.

To something that Abhiyansh asked, she replied, "when one aims precisely, you might get close. Aim vaguely and you get vague results." Abhiyansh looked up at her and then at the prints. Her work on his table showed her ability to see in-betweens and there was a tasveer too she had created, that of sign language between two people in the formal set-up of the discussion. Also, it revealed a very beautiful mind with a wide spectrum of contemplation.

Negi then called him outside. "Leaders do not create followers. They create leaders", Abhiyansh said and closed the discussion.

CHAPTER 4

Perspectives - getting to know others

How her career with me started - Abhiyansh:

Post the second fiasco Ria wasn't assigned a job. Negi and I were reviewing the selection of images from a shoot of a corporate building project. She was a novice looking into the Mac from behind our backs. The technical details of one section of the interiors were just not working out, lighting having not been properly planned in hindsight. Negi would snap at her whenever she spoke, which was quite frequent, to his displeasure. Technical settings, editing and software were Negi's expert areas. Gradually, he started ignoring her completely. A novice was supposed to stand on a side and observe. Listen too, maybe.

As a curator, Vayani had noticed Ria doing up a 'behind the scenes' on her own, in the preparation of an upcoming exhibition. Passing by, she asked Negi to assign her the same work. Negi complied with her, but not without a warning of 'not to trip' over anything, be absolutely quiet and damage nothing.

The results of the "behind the scenes" were used phenomenally by Vayani and won the appreciation of Negi too. Ria was the young imperfecto'. The "carefully crafted careless looks" with panache was natural to her and their work.

Negi and I both didn't deny a presence of paparazzi instincts to a certain degree in ourselves and in many we admired. The right moment as a photographer arrived when you were in harmony with the surroundings and the subject, whatever the situation. This girl had an excellent personal connection with people at large. I was drawn to her curiosity. She was a natural street photographer by disposition and was training herself for 'building photography'. Life, as a reflection of situations and the beauty of it, came naturally to her beautiful and yet untainted mind.

*****

Daring and congenial, a great blend. Do not change, he found himself saying aloud to her once.

Patience was an operational requirement, more than a trait and missing in many, he often said. Tall, boots, bandana, strong hands, easy laughter, broad frame lugging huge weights of equipment, he ventured out with his team. And the team, including Ria, set out on their jobs.

The highly reflective stretched ceiling announced the grandeur of the foyer. The rustic looking, reclaimed-wooden benches on the immaculately shining floor were moved at desired angles. And the panelling in the elevation too had the dissimilitude between the veneers, which spoke of the skin and wondrous texture of oak trees, against the high gloss polished surfaces and patina of leather.

In the formal area details like the weave of the fine ikkat patterns on the cushions had to be highlighted. Its inverse side with the chevron pattern, now dulled, and colour of the fabric wall panel was similar to the bold zig-zag streak running through the width of the rug. This was noted too. If one looked around for cues, the whole story in the interiors, as a correlation, could be read.

In the setup of the stands and lighting the views were identified so as the reflections and shadows were both sharp. Props in the setting to achieve the desired ambience and to hide snags were established. The architecture and interiors in design had as much to do with light as much as our trait, Abhiyansh said, holding his full-frame camera.

It was a new experience and Ria was in awe of the interiors and still more with the synergy of the shoot. She was a handy assistant as if by instinct, to Abhiyansh along with the others.

The next shoot was on the adobe construction. All natural, the silence of the building on the large site maintained as is, unobtrusively phenomenal. It even grew on the crew, speaking softly and soaking in the charm of the spaces. Like the silent notes in the flow of music, where you could sense the music in its completeness. The lack of corners was soothing, both inside and outside and exuded the warmth of a welcome. The mosaics, out of broken mirrors, were hemmed in the mud plaster. When the architects would have worked with the masons, the hands must have moved on their own, sculpting and blending with nature and with materials. The levels led into flowing continuation of walls, not ending at the corners as if more by intuition than by initial planning.

The surprise element was being on the slightly domical rooftop that was covered with grass which, from a satellite above, it would have looked as if it was a green patch in a forest. Abhiyansh had taken only two assistants so as not to be too intrusive in the private residence that it was and was to shoot in the daylight. Ria was sitting on the ledge holding her own camera, on the raised mud platform with a rounded off edge, at the angular staircase and did that here and there as much as the breaks in the shoot allowed.

Abhiyansh could hardly use her as an assistant this time. He ended up clicking her as a human model for scale in certain pictures. This was a real smart house, not bizarre in the name of smart.

When Ria discussed the kind of architecture's effect and style from the two shoots and the protocol employed for each by the team, he took out pictures of one of his projects from the folders in his tall rack. Here Abhiyansh kept the prints of selected images. The living room was full of art, collections of stones and leaves from various places but not blaring in the eye. No element in the frame seemed extra, neither the space in background or foreground.

Another one had the white Belgian lace on the white cushions, setting the tone of attractiveness and fragility, by a set-up of an umbrella bouncing off the light and with minimal shadows, except for the ones with the lace pattern.

Abhiyansh:

I asked for her portfolio, from before her joining, which I hadn't seen. The pictures from the rain series were on my table. She had captured from her heart, not from the head. The creative amplitude was strong and the technical inputs were haywire. She had a great ability to capture the "moment" where the entire composition came out as a story. It definitely reached a high level of being, in alertness. Pre-visualisation makes you an evolved artist, but the mavericks were what ….. I couldn't process the thought when she jumped in.

*****

The long conversation stimulated both of them. This girl did know rain and knew it well. She was much more intelligent and knowledgeable and possessed a deeper persona than how she came across as.

Picture of a national leader from the past, printed on an archival paper in 1:1 scale, as demanded by a university, was in front of him. 'Humanity and photography' he was preparing notes on the same for the University. He inspired everyone to be cosmopolite instead of being a traveller. For himself too it had been humbling, post journalism- the jungles, Aica, teaching.

There was always an option of going on but to live for higher pursuits and achievement, an ambition, which could be of various kinds, was what made it worth living. He taught people to open themselves up to life. He started looking forward to his conversations with her and each time churned out enough food for thought for her too.

November was seemingly the best time for a photographer to take a walk, the camera didn't quite like the dust that settled around. The morning rush of the school children and their buses, the rumpled leaves and sand piles hindering them from keeping up the pace with the parents, the average blue collared Indian's quick gait and the notorious looking drivers, there was enough to watch. Except for a few slow gardeners and chatty domestic helps, the battlefield of the road looked okay to amble towards the forest. The breeze worked well to add a zing to her feet.

CHAPTER 5

Aarija

The daze and haze sometimes makes it clear

The bike ride dampened all the other sounds, even of her singing. Just the numbing wind on the face, whizzing and howling past the ears, freeing up Ria's hair and at whim, flying and tangling. And views of a drenched village post the rain on all sides! The entire span of earth visible was well doused.

Ria had accompanied her to the farm. It was wonderful to "just be" with Aarija. After a usual bike ride alone, she had offered Ria a pillion ride and suggested Ria took off the aviators and exposed her eyes, to which she complied with reluctance. Post the ride without the helmet and soaked in the serene beauty of silvery patches of water on the road and drenched mud walls, fresh green of trees and lush fields, Ria was exuberant.

Aarija settled on deepened brown, dried fallen branches amongst the leaves, near the eucalyptus trees looking into nowhere, holding the brown fruits fallen nearby in her hand. The entire length of the non-metalled road bordering the orchards was lined with tall eucalyptus trees, silvery hued trunks standing as guards.

Aarija's belief was in nature, as one's belief is in prayer. Ria tilted her head upwards amidst those tall trees with Aarija. The white, bluish-green, flaky sepias and all colours in between looked unspoilt, just like Aarija. One didn't know whether you were wasting time with her or spending it. With her, wasn't it a neutral consciousness? And then it could become compulsive, like "let's waste time" if it came to that. Her eyes were unmixed- spoke of nothing, yet everything, should one want to seek. Your own goodness in a way reflected in her eyes.

She was the subject of an environmental portrait the next day. Of a village belle, with the charm of freshness and wisdom of ancestors in her head! The next portrait was against the green leaves, a close cut, and an intimate connection with the person's face. Not the entire face like Bryon Peterson's work.

The influence of an imagery Aarija carried, was a scene from her teenage, the one that she was describing, sitting on a low pile in her lemon georgette attire. On her way home in a bus, she saw a man afar emerging from the fields after having set crop stubble ablaze. That is a traditional way of clearing the field and the farmer was walking towards the road, away from the fire at a habitual pace. The sun had set and the silhouette of the man against the fiery colours and swaying flames behind, she couldn't forget. That gave her an impression of how nature was unfathomably strong but man in his own small ways could harness nature and vice versa.

Though she grew up to understand the repercussions of the stubble-burning act on the environment later but the metaphor remained with her, about her understanding of the phenomenal relationship of nature and man. An equation of balance! And of power!

Her voice spoke of clear promises, ones that she had made to herself. Promises of goodness amidst reluctance, repression, non-ownership, opposition, even if within the family or her college or society. Constant cleaning of emotional mess in the household had aged her more than her years.

Lacking a role model, she beat her own records and had herself to retort to. People's inherent behaviour returns to their inbuilt deep persona- situations make them react differently and a little normalcy brings them back to where they initially were. She could break this pattern- think other perspectives, fight, be strong, bend, but sometimes be left drained out too. Ria, without disturbing her contemplation, captured her in a frame. And then they retraced the route to shoot what they had been witnessing earlier.

A fortnight earlier, Ria had entered the discussion room in the office while the discussion was on the depth of field. She was explained "the viewfinder doesn't like you being careless. It doesn't like you to cut people randomly." "But I was capturing the expressions" she said. "What about your understanding of body language, right expression and the connections in relation to the scene?" The stress was on "in relation "and "the processed image of the same" retorted Abhiyansh.

She was asked to learn the importance of creative expenditure in the making of a tasveer. And to wait, watch and then click. To watch out her location and relate it to the scope of the shoot. Later she was summoned to Negi's cabin and assigned to click people and their expressions instead of covering the next conference. Pictures, that they could print in their publication. She was to expose herself to street photography in a professional way. She was to go travel in villages and breathe with the villagers and bring the experience back through her lens. So, she thought about her mom's long-standing wish to accompany her to the town. Maybe it was time to see some country life.

Assignment:

Results great looking in a go had to be well worked out in the detail. Intelligence as an equilibrium between minds making you conscious and heart marking surrender! The assignment would determine what parameters would be required to do justice to the purpose. Opening up to possibilities, respecting the balance but picking up from the variation in a controlled manner, with practice would make it so.

These photographs were not about facts. The "I" of the photographer in this assignment was important. His perspective, what he chose to show rode over the objectivity, controlled with points of reference. Balance was the driver of his frames.

For her, it was still the emotions, subjects who spoke through sentiments in her frames. She was encouraged by the studio to bring the same. But learn to spread her wings.

Whatever happened to the dispassionate ways of compiling factual reality

And see words differently

"You choose how to look at the world.

I chose not to look at it in a very clever way".

She had retained her vision-nice and simple.

Ria's faith was in people and love around, as much as in the unseen God.

To expose her to the larger perspectives and open-mindedness, she had been constantly sent to explore with assignments of various kinds, like a human sponge for learning. Assignments were gradually about the striking balance of the lines with the rest, not necessarily on the street.

And here was Aarija!

Ria reflected that she didn't want to meet Aarija again post this trip – she was such a righteous and serious person. You couldn't get to her easily, only she could get to you when she wanted, such was her circle of influence. Undertaking the tedious task of a little visionary amongst old stranded minds and standing by the change makers. Soothsayers did not tell destiny- she did. An extended family, living together, where everyone in the family thought was doing a bit more than his share of taking care of everyone and bearing the brunt. Her room in the Haveli was too full of heirlooms and stuff deemed obsolete, retrieved from being sold off.

Her book rack was at the corner, made of the slices of old deodar wood and books resting at an angle of the slant … The books were the ones bought by her uncles and aunts in their journeys and of herself, whenever she went to the A grade cities. A collection of cassettes and an old black telephone, brass, silver pots and embroideries and a whole cupboard of family heirlooms, a radiogram and what not.

The overall geometry of the exposed brick haveli was purely rectilinear. The huge door, pier, mouldings, chajjahs getting repeated in the same proportions created an internal harmonious rhythm. The doors carved out of huge logs, the ceilings with generous wooden joist roofs, and patina of deodar almost a century old. The pursuing of restoration was nowhere in question, with too many stakeholders and too many troubles.

The family was warm and hospitable. Much emphasis was laid on the correct positioning of the cutlery and crockery wasn't repeated on the table for the first two days.

On the third morning, the whole household seemed different. Something was wrong. The high-pitched voices were different-more towards alarming. The high-dosed active family was on a still higher dose of flurry today with their temperaments.

There was a power cut!

Random power cuts were a normal phenomenon in the towns of India and such conditions could clearly alter the temperaments.

The water was being poured into large vessels for heating. For head washing, Aarija was demanding that the soft water be heated separately, instead of the hard water. There could be no ironing of clothes as well. For that, the generator would require diesel. After the diesel was sent for, with much humdrum and clamour- the generator asked for a little repair that morning. That set the escalation in tempers a little higher. After most of the first half of the day had gone by, the household seemed ready for a start and with an adjusted temperament.

Ria gathered from the mali, that the play-out of this phenomenon was nothing in comparison to the play-out when summers are at their peak.

With her gear, she accompanied the elder brother of the house to the farm some 20 km away, on an overcast day. There was something about the fog here that felt as if distilled droplets were suspended in the freshest of air. And one wanted to inhale those deeply. His little daughter came along, carrying her tiny bag. They halted on the way when a poplar tree plantation took a fancy to Ria's eyes.

The rammed earth boundary wall was an irregular shape, dropping to the eye level to peep inside at places and with two levels of barbed wire as a restraint, looked interesting. Through the gate with horizontal metal bars, she shot a hunched old man warming himself up with fired up wood. She entered the gate and focused on the rest and lo! Behold- it was breathtakingly beautiful in an imperceptible way and she gasped.

There were neat rows of poplar trees, thousands of them, upright, of similar height, planted in a grid, the foliage too having spurted from matching levels, much above your head. The slender built of trunks reached a good forty feet or more and vanished into the fog along with their delicate branches. The hue of foliage changed from few leaves of green to most of lemon, to ochre and then of pale orange, crowning tall above. Overall the jolly ochre hue in the backdrop of haze not only made up for the sunless day, it added a heavenly charm. The diminishing distance and colour made up for excellent perspective shots. The ground was thickly covered with large sized leaves, multiple times the number of those intact on the fragile looking branches. Pale and dark and all shades between burnt sienna and dull brown, tinged with a bit of grass and grey crunched ones hither and thither. There was a thick layer of mulch, so much so that you couldn't feel the ground under and saw white birds pecking in it with their beaks.

As a matter of fact leaves were continuously falling, at their own pace, in their own frolic trip. She quickly adjusted the setting to WB and got lost in the serendipity of capturing the moment. She wanted to take mental images too as her fingers and eyes were absorbed in the Canon.

The experience was being etched in a corner of her heart where only seraphic got stored. The bearded old man looked at them with a kind of indifference, which only a villager sitting on the ground, wrapped in a shawl, turbaned head, warming his hands by the fire, can. That indifference was not out of rudeness or a non-welcoming thought. It was a perfect acceptance of you as a fellow human being.

The brother sat with the old man, on his feet and spread out his hands for warmth. No words were exchanged. The daughter went towards the swing hanging from the sturdy tree branch near the hut by the gate. A little girl with lovely bronze coloured matted hair wearing a red salwar-kameez peeped from the edge of the mitti wall, behind which was a hut. Ria called her out. She didn't shy away or exhibit a facial reaction; just came outside and stood beside the swinging stranger. An experience of quite a lot, in reticence!

Ria walked towards the poplars, where the meticulous grid planted at an angle was more conspicuous, for the plots are not always perpendicularly cut from the road. A white bird as a blessing, punctuated her frame in the right two third with the trees centred vertically. Another one flew and she upped her speed with the clicks and followed the movement of now a flock of white birds. Few of these images would be deemed locked status, she was certain.

Only when you are comfortable in your own skin, do you enjoy the rest. Well, I would make my own little setting or may be a big one, she revelled humorously. When you are overcome with your best, you are complete in yourself. Contemplating so, her camera zoomed to capture the fall of a single leaf, having relished its span on the tree, now gladly enjoying the journey to earth in a dancing zig-zag fall, taking its own sweet time in the breeze. It met with multitudes of leaves on the ground, most of them damp. Ria's state of mind harmonized with this place and she got images of shadows, foliage, and the slow calm.

The trees and the breeze hummed a more noticeable sound. By the end of the visit, the brother called his daughter, took out her hair adornment and clipped them in the village girl's matted hair-just like that- again no talk, no fuss, no celebration, no cheer, no reaction from anyone. Only the little daughter said, "Dad, I have thousands of hair clips."

Ria came out from the iron gate carrying a lot more beauty in her heart than she had entered with. She looked back at the five to six acres of heaven, a small family by the gate and white birds flying around at a low level. The time frame was fuzzy and irrelevant, the span of the day there, completely coherent. The three of them sat in the jeep and started, again in silence. He was the same man who in the morning was shouting at home, Ria pondered over. May be so many of these pure hearted people were living together- some space was missing from each other when they all shared the confines of the big house. In their own space they were all amiable.

While listening to someone with compassion, you might not relate to it at the same time. The strongest of the people are judged when they have a weak time. Traditionally the adversaries' approach and attack at such times.

The same is possible even in a family. Somebody needed to tell this girl that it was all right to be imperfect. Overdoing things has a different Pandora box kind of a knack of its own. She was a friend with a German girl virtually connected who, while being a student in a university, was travelling the world. She would share her opinions about the destinations and knew India mostly for corruption. On her visit to a high-profile wedding in Delhi, she had witnessed local songs and customs being played with galore. The same folk songs and the ritual of dancing with a pot of fire on the head, which were dying in the village, were being replaced with DJs from the cities. Ria wanted to revive such arts and rituals. Taking others along in the pursuit was the battle.

What is ludicrous/ ignorable for one could be an art form for another. Luxury and abundance bring awareness with them and of course, confidence, Aarija stressed.

Together, the pattern that you build will not be acceptable to your next set of generations. Break patterns too. Few elderly people in some families understand and imbibe these as a form of tradition or gracious planning or dictatorship. Aarija wanted to maintain the patterns, which were graceful and imbibed external influences in them.

To change the light to a positive one around you, the guru reminds you in time of changing the lens. Her guru was herself for now. The guru hadn't revealed yet but she was on the path to that revealing and, in the journey, searching herself.

"And how is it that you do everything in such a stylish way?" Ria asked.

"O as a child" she said "when I was taught, I was taught holding needles in a certain way so that the fingers in the process looked elegant, even if that reduced the knitting speed." Those made her learn forever how to hold her tools with panache first.

Ria came across an old collection of her father's and extended family pictures, fiddling through the bookrack. They were a black and white treasure trove. Mahattas in Connaught place had clicked a portrait of everyone in the family. As it went, for everything from shopping to availing medical facilities, the family members travelled all the way to New Delhi in the past.

Mahattas - Ria made a note to check them out.

The assignment back to Delhi consisted of images of a slice of expertise seeping in Ria and emerging out in print. Negi looked at her and looked at the image in his hand. Of a thin framed old villager, one hand under his turbaned head and another one on his chest, lying on a cot and looking up expressionless and of a tiny girl in red ol' ethnic dress and half a cow in the left, a very tight frame. And he gazed again at Ria with a thoughtful look.

Encouraged, enriched with abundance! How important was it to witness abundance in childhood. Abundance in perception! Not grow under pressure; if there were any complex that would spurt up, it would be superiority. The attitude of doing it right till you learn to diagnose and determine your own right and wrong. And surrounded by beauty and aesthetics, her father never came back home without carrying flowers for her. She told people about Aarija in her office.

YOU, my friend, are extra ordinary.

We – dear friend are most ordinary, simple and beautiful. The world is nuts

But then, we like nuts!

Ria and Aarija had arranged for poplar plants, which were essentially long sticks of about ten feet, to be sent to Delhi. Ria had identified a large patch behind the studio and wanted to surprise everyone. Abhiyansh got angry at this plan. He took Ria outside and explained. "This area of mustard wasn't planted by us; it was a leftover patch from the large mustard fields existing earlier. The ecosystem of a place, the fauna inherent to geographical conditions, was important" he said. So was history.

It was important to maintain tradition. What you did in Rome along with the Romans, sometimes had to be left there itself, relinquished on the way back home.

The poplars were duly sent back in a canter along with a printed album for Aarija by the office. And sent along with it was an appreciation letter for the permission to publish her personal pictures.

Even much later, the remembrance of the time spent with Aarija transported Ria to the rain drenched fields. The memory of tall eucalyptus lined in perspective on the left with foliage rumpling down around the smooth white trunk covering half of her frame, sun rising from behind, creating slanting shadows diagonally across the frame, interspersed with soil smoothened post rain, the lower right greened out in depth, a crow perched on the thin concrete post holding the barbed wire and the top right evenly blued out with tiny waffling white clouds.

Ria thought of her on outdoor shoots. She would be biking. On roads dry and washed clean post rain and with the evenly blue sky and electric wires reflecting in the freshly collected puddles. The mud wall would be dry too with just the top and bottom wet layer bordering it and all hues of coloured English roses visible behind, the dried leaves and humus on the sides of the road merged in the freshly soaked soil. And her bike would be leaving a trail behind.

Two of Ria's images in print found a place in a box file in Abhiyansh's book rack. Money and patrons weren't important to her yet, the honesty in her work was. If only she didn't change!

The Wall.

Abhiyansh:

I was away for few hours. The labour was moving debris out of my office premise. The wall had simply vanished! No wall at all. Gone in a matter of hours. Whatever happened!

Ria:

The dampening on the wall had dried but the junctions of the painted surface and glass panel had suffered

damage. It was in a dilapidated state, as per Abhiyansh.
He was unable to use it as a crimson background and it
irritated him to enter the office and see his much-
cherished work booth on the left in not-so-perfect a
state.

After a futile attempt to trace the artist who had worked
on the wall, Negi had roped in a designer specializing in
infusing retail spaces with art. He discussed at length the
troubles involved in support issues, junctions, false
ceiling and several other constraints they would face
while redoing it. The hour-long discussion didn't
conclude anywhere, in fact a thick cloud of confusion
seemed settled in the air, unnerving me as I was trying to
stack catalogues in order.

I had come to the studio on a holiday to study in the
studio library. On the adjacent plot with an ongoing
construction, the contractor could be heard shouting at
the labour. I stood there watching the contractor, who
despite his demeanour looked friendly. It was as if the
labour's on-off switch operated through his harsh words
and the decibel level of his voice. Boss was away to
finalise the details of an assignment and Mr Negi was
nowhere around.

I struck off a conversation with the contractor. Not only
was he decent in his conversation, he was pretty well
read. I showed him the wall, discussed in detail,
understood how the wall was not hampering the
structural system of the old building and the false ceiling
had enough bracing from the ceiling and would need only
a bit of repairing and track lights repositioned. Then I
explained to him why it was important to knock it down
immediately and offered to pay in advance. He smiled

and whistled to his man Friday who looked like a supervisor.

They wanted the electrician to cut the wire before carrying on with their work. It wasn't part of their job. The supervisor got the tools and cut it himself and left.

The three labourers that the contractor sent blanked out at operating without the on/off switch. So, he came back in at quick intervals and in four hours the malba was out of the office.

Late in the evening, the boss walked into the library. Everything was usual. He got his cappuccino, picked up his paper, and adjusted the angle of the pen on his diary. No word was uttered about the wall. I hadn't felt anxious, neither had I anticipated how he would react. The evening went through smoothly as any other day. I never bothered, even later. If I did, I would imagine him narrating it as one of his dinner stories, a good conversationalist that he had always been.

All that I knew at that moment was that I felt sure, sure of myself. Now there wouldn't be any technical glitches to be discussed, only the details about how to implement the new design.

In the following days too, he never did really look at the wall, as it seemed, no shouting, freaking out, detailing it further or anything about it. Kind of behaved as if the wall hadn't existed. Only the interior designer wasn't called in again and God knows who designed the next enchanting wall. The day it was complete, was just like another day and he started using the background for shoots.

A series of images on the construction workers, construction materials, scaffoldings and ropes came out like a story from the apprentice who was idle, in the long lunch hour. Again, a delight for Vayani and a disapproval from Mr. Negi for waste of time and resources.

Robert Capa's book said if you are close enough, your pictures are not good enough. Wait for a moment in the place and connect- the connection will show in the images you made and it did show. The resource directory got the writers' knack into the team as they forayed in the creative journey.

"Everybody has an innate action to perform in the dance. Who are we to declare about somebody's wrong move? We have our own graceful moves to make. How can we stop the formation He above is watching and playing? "Ria wrote in her diary.

For we are so quick in judging!

He may be on a cross road himself, or on a path unknown. To really know him walk with him, be a companion till he finds familiar grounds.

Abhiyansh 's self-assurance reflected in his behaviour. Discussing a picture, he would come up with a description of the situation, sometimes in a single word. Some pictures even got him interested in deep belly laughter, infecting everyone to open up to the lighter side of the visuals.

He was going over the recent assignment with the young team over the results of just-shot portraits and gave profuse instructions about post- processing. Now Ria was absorbing the nuances, like a sponge. She had accompanied him for this modelling assignment that required a multitude of assistants. Her job that day was to manage the flexi in order to reflect the light off as required. The catch light in the eyes was to be facilitated along with the shoulder blades.

The portraits on the screen were tremendously larger than life, frozen moments in advance, between the connection of the subject and the viewer. An element of the subject as desired, was enhanced through an expression or a unique treatment. At times it was also about depicting the subject's work, environment, relationships, fantasies, mood or other characteristics. They captured the essence of his life in his body, one-life or alternative lives he is leading. Metaphorically, multiple overlaying compiled in one.

The schedule was on everyone's desk for the next project. Ria could be used as a senior assistant for this assignment, considering her ardency in the previous shoot.

Abhiyansh stationed his gear in the atria. This space was an engaging fusion of functions applying to the nature of work, just as the meaning of Atria, the heart. With the floor plates wrapping around the triple height, the courtyard acted as an activator and was an activated space itself. There was a renewal of purpose through those shared and participatory spaces. It was a visual link between floors and the daylight was welcomed into the entire space through it. It served as a major vantage point for the shoot. Through the portal, a series of lights were viewed at an angle. These pendant lights were akin to each other, not to the rest of the lighting. And when you walked towards the portal, your axis of movement was directed towards the vertical offset between these lights.

The brief thread of balance, picked neatly and gracefully without disturbing the frozen music of architecture, was only enhanced with some more notes. The movement through the space was pretty dynamic in pictures though. Another tripod was being set in another corridor, against the suspended lights, capturing the view of functional space.

The interiors here, so muted, integrated into the building so well. The overall extension of colour from one space to another was as graceful as the ballerina's shoe being the same colour as her stocking in order to extend or maintain the same line visually. Abhiyansh discussed this with his crew. When he spoke of ballet extended lines, the catch light in his own eyes became brighter.

For a span of a year and a half she delved in experiential learning.

"I saw enriched landscapes in front of me. Here I was searching for a point to rest my eyes", said Abhiyansh in his description of the image."

Abhiyansh taught; you are not close enough; your pictures of animals are not good enough. A picture was to be created, not to be clicked. A "tasveer" was to be made. Photography was an art form not as old as painting. And for the first time he gave an example of a colleague. That of Negi's.

Negi was known for his wildlife expeditions, photographer's patience, and dedication. The full frame camera, the specks of rain, the back lit photography of silhouettes of animals in their own habitat. The young leopard looked intently into the camera while walking towards it on the bark, fierce eyes popping out on the intruders. He made pictures that sucked you in. Tasveerein!

He spoke about Camera Obscura and the dark chamber's journey. The images of Kamara's dark room were on his picture wall.

There was a shake in one of the good compositions. The shutter speed had to be lowered, he explained. The flight of words missed Negi, he was reticent. He had a collection for anything to do with photography and the original prints. On his display niche was a signature moment of Abhiyansh captured while preparing to click a ballerina.

For human eye's reading of the contrast in a jiffy required the subject to be at the maximum contrast point. Stronger the contrast, stronger the attraction to the eye! So, the centre of interest in the frame was placed in the maximum contrast area and was to be shot through a relevant filter.

Her work earlier was more by intuition than by design. Abhiyansh assigned her to get trained with Negi for the next month knowing fully well that both would turn to him in exasperation. She would not set the camera and wait. An interesting event would catch the camera 's viewfinder.

In an assignment of clicking an ugly installation you could shoot a series of distinctive, repetitive elements held together by say a connector element. That element could be a hint, a colour, a balcony railing, a plane, and a feature. And make the pictures interesting.

You must know the rules and then bend them, Negi insisted. Just deciding to climb the Everest out of excitement without assessing the availability of resources and without training was a disaster to accompanying Sherpas directly and to many others indirectly, not to mention the harm on the environment. Creative expenditure to understand the rules was important.

Ria quickly lowered the ISO to adjust to the low light. Using brightness and contrast as the visual properties that made an object distinguishable from the background and scattering of light in order to deviate from a straight trajectory. The workshop was to understand and create superlative images. To negate the effect of reflection off metals, he asked her to borrow the polarizing filter from Shishdhar and shoot again. Portrait as a product used absorption of light- not reflection, refraction, or transmission. The silhouette Abhiyansh had created of Ria's favourite model was through scattering.

The maturity of skin glowed well in the picture-the tone and colour were articulated impeccably by the lighting. Rendered with the delicacy of watercolour.

Eyes were to be squinted in order to delete unnecessary details in this art. How the inner eyes work, how the unnecessary disappears when you conceive a frame.

She created an image interaction between the dancing girl and the interiors applying the "intersection of the thirds" and compositional shapes for the eye movement, so that the eye was attracted to where the photographer or for that matter as the artist wanted.

Camera was an extension of the arms. Abhiyansh just instructed the camera what he wanted to capture like the merger of creativity and calculation. His well-balanced compositions were easy on the eyes, the eyes followed a pattern he had conceived while framing and rested where he wanted. Ria had understood and applied it well. Pursuing excellence always excited her.

He spoke of the push pull sensation that keeps the eye moving around the image instead of the viewer's eye being led into the picture and displayed the exemplary work to his students too. Whether to follow or rebel against the rules, he said was dependent on the creative juices and the photographer's mood and instinct.

Like with a pen instead of pencil where you are forced to make a committed statement, Negi was of the view that the frames shot should be limited and experimental. Abhiyansh was of the contrary opinion -one could dwell on perceiving the view and improvise the scene and vision and take multiple shots. Like sketching. Photoshop, he said was like the darkroom processing, brushing with ingredients and then garnishing.

His resolute ways and just the sentence "already on the way back" whenever contacted made his presence never leave the office. A picture of him in black bandana and boots, a faded green jumpsuit camera around the neck and hands reaching out to something in front and a nearly dazed expression was displayed in Negi's work place next to his Praktica and Minolta from pre digital times.

DSLR though were better in terms of exposure and practical functioning but the old cameras were retained for old times' sake. You could imagine and know the result in a week and then save the precious film. Double exposure, triple exposure, rewind was accurate. 50mm 70-200 were his lenses for these.

Bela, the painter and Tarun, the tycoon's portrait, were assigned to Ria, but without an assistant. The shoot demanded her to check on their house a day prior. The extended deck was a suitable interconnected place in the country home. It provided some definition to the outdoor space- welcoming in gesture and in form through the inbuilt ledge- seating and add-on seating. It exuded a sense of well-being and satisfaction. But they wanted a portrait by the fireplace.

The quality of light in the room articulated the colour and texture of the finishes. The warm suffused glow on the stones and hearth in the late afternoon made up for the background. Painting too played more with the light; the artist had herself chosen the backgrounds.

Next day, framing the hearth while studying the effect of the lighting pattern falling on the face, searching the mid shadows and deciding to arrange light for the triangle or to go with the loop lighting, she involved the subjects in a sustained conversation.

Tarun, chic and comfortable and Bela, who possessed all the charm and poise in the world, was now getting conscious and started rambling. Her salt and pepper hair against the abstract art nouveau artwork looked wonderful.

The regularity and continuity sought by the eye was met by the strokes of brush if not by elements. The sunny smile in the suggestively suffused toned ochre scarlet mixed kind of orange glowed well. The livid base embedded in scarlet, almost lurid besides the grey hearth complimented the rosy blush of her cheeks. And a viridian hue oozing out of orange created a spell.

Ria suggested the lady wear an extended kaajal and she did go inside to oblige. Tarun was quite easy to fall in a conversation with. In terms of imaginative and creative input, the street photography and painting art vye with each other, Ria quoted Abhiyansh. Painting of course being the senior. Abhiyansh pressed them to get a creative punch in the street photography, something to set it apart from a usual frame. Painting in post modern and contemporary genres of imaginative input. The rhythm is everywhere. Nature likes it that way, the sky is, mountains are, childbirth is and even hurricanes and torpedoes and destruction.

While in photography, the natural frame was an asset, painting's journey to the surreal, to keep it as open to interpretations. A wild unicorn could run into the oblivion. Ria directed the conversation towards the topics that could put Bela into ease, vital for a homey atmosphere.

Painting turned out to be her intrinsic and uncared for passion realized only later he said and when Bela resumed her place besides the art works, joined in the conversation. She spoke about the revolution of the impressionists and soon her whole persona glowed up as the conversation inclined towards her paintings and all that inspired her journey. Painting was slower a journey in the mind and fix-its' like Photoshop/Lightroom were readily available in terms of ideas and paints. But the beauty didn't lie in it. Observing in the distance with your own eyes and dewdrops in the eyelashes blinking slowly or gazing into the soul of ideas or objects as well as people was inherent to a painting. And transcendence was a "means to it" as with the other art forms.

The use of colour and brush strokes flowing with the composition, in order to create a movement in the beholder's eyes and the co-relation simultaneously developing with the canvas was the artist's strength. Colours she said were the strongest potential holders as a base for visual experience. And understanding each colour was like understanding a friend's personality type and what mixed with the other could produce joy or vendetta.

Speaking about her work and then focussing on the camera she gave the look that Ria wanted.

Why her own house was a riot of colours then like a pandemonium when she understood the character and strength and individuality of them. It was like unrequited love, she said and a celebration of that. The riot according to her kept her agile and intoxicated, the soft hues and the bright, bold colours, their proportions and jugglery in her work, teased and calmed her down. In a sublime manner, devoid of pretentions, it summed up to pure joy of working. The closest she could relate that joy could be in the toiling of a day labour, when physical and mental energies conjure into one. Also, that kept her company in the absence of her husband who was a highflying corporate success. He was smiling away to glory, holding her snugly in a side hug and swaging a winning smile, well befitting.

The results were excellent this time and Negi remarked aloud that Ria could cut out the diamond aptly sometimes. The genuineness, empathy and warmth of this girl started popping out, a streak not to be ignored.

Bela's words reflected deeper in the eyes than the sound of them-as in classical dance. Her aura in general kept playing in Ria's head for a fortnight. It was like processing a potion gathered too quickly. How that sublime, strong character was leading a life less extraordinaire, Ria mulled on for long.

The role reversal in oneself may be is bound to happen. Grace and wisdom, love and patience one would sow and then reap. Or the negatives sowed. Be ready to get the same, your planted trail, she reflected. If it doesn't come from the other side in the same form, it will manifest in another way. So would faith and love- spurt up somewhere, someplace, sometime.

After the return from the hills with the entire studio, she ventured on her own. She was called to the studio for assignments though.

Assignments that she couldn't refuse!

The face of the railways was changing. Metro had marked and established its entry in New Delhi in the able hands of a strong personality, leading the project. The transport system was otherwise deemed to fail.

Her assignment was to cover the tracks of New Delhi as is and rendering them b/w. Even of people still daring to cross them along with the luggage.

She would make an effort to look chic in her everyday meetings. "What beautiful curls have you ordained yourself with today?" Tina, her friend exclaimed.

Oh, my hair straightener wasn't working!

Sumit loved the curls. And the dysfunctional straightener soon was put to rest.

"Did you like what your fiancé got for you?" Tina asked further.

"Yes, of course! If I had to pick a dress myself, I would have never picked that one. But then He got it for me, where was the question of not liking it? When I would wear and see appreciation in his eyes, I would love it."

Sumit called on his way to pick her up from the studio. She was sitting on the tree hump. "What were you thinking and why has the cat got your tongue?"

"O, I was thinking of the bricks of pineapple and strawberry laced ice-creams in the fridge at home. And of reaching home as early as possible"

Peals of Sumit's laughter! Her simplicity and transparency were compelling. And the hypnotizing maze of utopia!

Assignments kept coming in, wherein she outdid herself. Each time. 'Desire is the basis of achievement, why would she compromise or decline. Mendacious it might be and will end, why not live it. Accept all different kinds of worlds.'

Plopped on the canned furniture pepped up with red cushions, diary in lap, the heavy grey of sky forming a stunning backdrop against the luxuriously swaying fresh new green leaves of Gulmohar, in the month of March. To charm the contemplative occupant below! The spread of radiating slim, open armed twigs as graceful as just manicured out of nail spa seemed to be enjoying their own dominance over music. The clouds stirring at an easy pace, enjoying their own tune. Metronome set for the entire scenery.

Only the wires jutting out leading to the junction boxes in the street were horrid and a nuisance for most of the pictures. But they had to be composed in a way so that they added tension in the frame for the sociological impact of the images.

She saw him arriving and changed the lens. Playing on a loop was the music heard from their common list. Sumit was trying to scare away the pup. The pup was in no mood to give up, kept following till he reached the staircase. Now Sumit wasn't in a mood to give up. He encouraged the pup to take a jump at each step. Hop-hop, it slowly followed Sumit to the door. Ria got some bread from inside and Sumit fed it to the bundle of soft fur.

On the laptop screen was the recent chat..

What did you imagine

Making love to you, in the hills

O my, I will fall in love with you

..........Of course you will.

There was loud barking outside the door. Sumit opened the door to find his pup returned with a whole set of dogs. Ria got the rest of the packet of bread and this time Sumit had to go drop the tiny wilful pup that wasn't ready this time to jump down on the steps.

The box of lenses he had got from Chandni chowk was on the table. His gifts on special occasions were lenses, gadgets and props until Ria started asking for an armful of flowers. And that too an arrangement of just one or two blending colours in an aesthetic arrangement, a definite no to the multi-coloured bouquets. She would set the music and lay flowers on the table over food of his choice. A nourishing friendship!

"I will miss u in my dreams today."

"What will you do with me?"

"Let the dreams decide."

They got married after a brief courtship over chats and in person. Any differences identified by the world in culture, thought process or other parameters, they decided to do away with and build a future on their own.

In Britain!

CHAPTER 6

The transition, London

The story is for those who reflect, otherwise it just passes by!

So used to working up minds in India, being idle in that well sorted-out house, her brain kept cooking ideas to put herself to some use. Even buying those super discounted chocolates with their shelf life ending fast gave a tiny bit of satisfaction of doing something. Every time she walked through the chor-gali, she was tempted to sell her new silk grey scarf with dull silver motifs and a handicraft bag carried along from India. And the verbal maths calculated a profit off few INR and then reconverted to pounds.

The massive apartment on the fourth floor, located at old street was warm and comfortable, given the nature of harsh British winters. Outdoors, the chill got to the bones. Out of the country for the first time, she was equally enchanted in the day but lonely by the dark setting in the evening, sepia to grey to ash. Sumit on his return from the office perpetually found her waiting outside, shivering. A familiar face was just so welcoming for her.

All through her life, having woken up by the jolt that is sunlight, instead of a clock, the day here started rather slow with lazy rays of damp sun, if any. The precious sunlight abandoned the city by four pm, so did her cheerful energy. The gleam in the eyes that comes with a purpose and resolute steps was kind of elusive here.

Sumit's office was near the London Museum, which soon became her almost daily afternoon haunt. Other days she saw herself rushing through the museums and her evenings would seek smell and sounds that were familiar. Standing on the platform, waiting for the tube was like being in the setting of a novel with a tall, red hair ravishing girl in long boots and a debonair man, standing nearby with an i-pod. The sounds of whooshing trains and almost none of the people, the dark alleys in the metro stations and the roads with tactile and cycle tracks, the crisp signage.

An order prevalent everywhere-this world was charmingly different, which she captured in pictures, life on streets as offered. Christmas was approaching, Oxford Street was humming, Angel had new lights. There was a buzz of activity everywhere, yet the heart longed for the sun and warmth.

The restoration work with the scaffolding hidden by the full-scale graphic of St Peter's Cathedral Basilica, printed on flex on 1:1 elevation, without hampering the city vista impressed her too whenever she crossed by.

Busking was one of the best experiences. The musicians with their pianos and cellos by the roadside were a spectacle. Ria was mesmerized by these artists and spellbound by their performances. Gradually she picked up the custom prevalent there. Courtesy seemed to be the norm and the smartness of well-dressed pedestrians wooed her too. Of smiling at a stranger, a random remark about the weather.

The red telephone booth and the cobbled stone paving appeared in so many of her photographs. Allured by them along with roadside, transport systems and infrastructure, she stood an entire day in front of one of the booths as a prop and observed morning to evening transition in the vibrancy. Of the various kinds of visitors, change in behaviour of booth-users captured as the day passed by. A series of stories going by!

She clicked the most unusual of shoes in one of the show windows and the usual ones on the streets, a riot of colours, shapes, material, bizarreness, and finesse. Only if she could find someone wearing the show window ones and add to her imagery of the different sorts of people wearing those. As soon as she went to an area frequented by a lot of people, she would start feeling cheerful. Covent Garden, Oxford, the history museum, science museum got the better of her.

The overwhelming grandeur of the circular space at the British Museum, the vibe of the scale of the space in white and the glazing unified were sensory relieving.

Britain had a rich culture, heritage and history. But somewhere the spirituality and the connection that one gets used to by its embedding into one's own self, was missing.

She couldn't connect to the environment in general as liveable. Even in these times of goodness, there was a kind of a void, a reminder of what was truly important, missing. Just like the symphony, which you can't understand but is enjoyable. And sometimes even better, for the same reason. And this one definitely had more than a chord missing.

Ambling she came by an area clinic with a few moms standing outside for smoke and kids playing inside. A man about to check in to admit himself stopped by and over random conversation told her that the children inside had come for a regular check-up of growth, provided by the state. She had noticed that babies here cried far lesser than the babies in India. Also amusing was witnessing a random lady the other day scolding a stranger with a baby in a stroller for being outdoors at dinnertime. The baby ought to have been shoved in the bed, the furious lady said and provided Ria with an expression of a bewildered adult.

The other morning Sumit and Ria went for a stroll around their block. Sumit waved to a man arranging the garbage bags outside the main entrance. The neighbourhood was unfrequented this early and Sumit pointed out all the fancy cars in the block he was fond of. One Z4, a two-seater in black stood above the rest. Ria asked about the person in overcoat and hat to whom Sumit had waved to and it was bewildering to know that he was the owner of the building.

We live in a cacophony in India, she told a stranger on the bus and that was what the brain perceived normal. Now she looked for strangers in the bus who were open to conversations. For a specially challenged person, the exit gate was lowered. Back home in India, one gets so used to the voices around, the noise of chiselling, the continuous metal clanking, the old Hindi song playing at an odd job ironing guy's station, chirping of birds, squirrels, random conversations in the streets, irritating horn of all sorts perceivable in the distance. She felt nostalgic about the reassuring whistle of a pressure cooker at home. And only if she could walk by a stick stand of sweet potatoes on the roadside and get a whiff of the aroma in the cold, cold December evening!

Here it was abnormally silent, punctuated by mechanical sounds, the retail shops closing by 5 pm. The apartment was silent and the corridors outside were cold in ambience. The emptiness of the linear connectors of apartments and the absence of natural light throughout the day was misanthropic. The worst was the screeching of patrolling police cars in the middle of the night or in the morning wee hours as a routine. Again the Indian mind was attuned to those sounds as some warning or unwanted situations.

Two mornings of the week when Jessa came to change linens and vacuum clean the apartment as a company provided facility, the apartment felt warmer. The

Philippine student was the mother of a toddler who was entrusted to the husband when she stepped out of the house. She offered a lift to Ria one day in her car and that was a warm offer of keeping a company she was now used to.

Sumit's boss came the other day to pay her weekly salary at their apartment, which was overdue. Sumit and Ria hastily prepared a meal and were a little offended when he didn't touch a thing served on the table. Maybe he too was offended, by their insistence.

Outside the Buckingham, on a cold, cold day she would go check out the price of coffee on the cart, calculate the conversion in rupees and drop it repeatedly. The coffee was 25 times the price in India. But then that day was horribly chilly and by the time she enquired for the price of a mere slice of a rice cake, her mind had gone numb with calculations and the chill. She eventually bought it. Sumit was standing on a side watching her, not wanting to spend on him and not stopping her, graciously.

This kind of equation created an attitude of "gracious discomfort". She wished they both spent together and restricted sometimes. But then they learnt gradually to enjoy the differences in preferences. That of spending too!

The walk with double caps on the head over the earmuffs, thick layer of an overcoat over layers of clothing minus the camera, towards the Palace had to be continued. That explained the country's obsession about stepping out of the house only after checking the real feel factor in the news. British comedy about the weather didn't sound so much of comedy now. Concluding the walk was important in order to make memories, for the memory to filter out the physical discomfort of the chill and retain the walk in other sensory perception, such as the dazed beauty of vast landscapes on an axis towards an impressive building, as in a digital walkthrough or only better.

Sumit did shoot a few pictures. The landscape in the foreground will have to be touched, she thought, without pointing the finger, not desiring to lose an iota of heat and not saying it aloud for the same reason. Add the touch-up on Photoshop or the newbie that was Lightroom will remove the faint shadow the tripod would produce, she forethought. Sometimes it was better to use the pre-sets of Lightroom than using the controls of your gadget in hand. But she had no wish of discussing this with the husband who had warm hands and opening her own mouth would mean further lowering of body temperature.

So, after centuries of cruelty and manipulating the dignity of our nation and horrendous suffering unforgivable, had the British not left us with Lutyen's Delhi, Parliament house on a bigger scale than their renowned Palace of monarchy? This conclusion and the experience of the views of the landscape in fathomable lower degree by the hour measured on Celsius scale, was totally worth the while.

As time passed by slowly in her everyday cribbing, Sumit sent her packed one late evening to admire and capture the Tower Bridge. The unusual skyscraper, forty stories of fragility held in glass, lest the egg it was shaped as, slime down or become a sliced egg. All sorts of contorted and amusing ideas floated through her but she also stood transfixed, admiring the sheer beauty of the curved marvel and evolution of the historic city from the other side of the tower bridge. And she returned in haste, conditionally thinking about her most conservative uncle in India and about returning home before the night set in.

As she tired of being on her own, he started accompanying to drop her to the entrance of a few places now and then in the morning or during his lunch break in a city where one could be on his own otherwise, logistically speaking, with maps, data and assistance available everywhere. In the Somerset house, he stood for a while with her and then left.

Can bliss be preached? Yes it could be- a collective force of bliss-this captivating female in front of her was the emanatory of it to the outside world. Her arms jingled and in tandem with the joy shared with the rest of the group. She was the reason why Christmas giving and sharing becomes happiness for so many around. With giving of joy, a collected pre ordained force of many, reverberating the entire phenomenon.

The face of this female in her prime with wavy blonde hair, around whom the queue seemed to have formed, was a thoroughly absorbing visual. The whole family or may be family friends too, in a series of dozen arms interlocked on both her sides, were on the ice rink, skating under the sky. She did not make pictures out of it; the episode resonated with her for a very long time. Of the entire scene, she could forever remember the female's glimmering laughter and the whole group around in joyous synchronisation.

And she would remember how she forgot to make a tasveer out of it, submerging herself in the beauty of it!

Why get out of college predicting everybody as per their achieved grades, only to collide into a senior later, the one who looked laze queen in the making, in the yesteryears. The same person was transformed into a hardworking, core cut professional with a cold steel glance, sitting across you in an eatery. It was a delight to Ria to come across an old mate in a café and a relatable face. Then Ria showed her some of the prints of her work. Those of brick bollards, of streetlights, kiosks by the side, of cornices.... Of the blank ground floor, the greens climbing up, warmed up by white balance, in candescent WB, a jargon the friend wouldn't have understood. Never the less, Ria went on with ferocity.

Sumit had got the prints of her clicks from the airport too. Her first international flight in a wide body range aircraft. And as chance would have it, Jet had just launched it. It was as just enough and handsomely lit in warmth, muted hues and welcoming grandeur, like an elegant living room. The fascinating strips and array of lighting, flight of long stairs and without a landing to the aircraft. And the experience of ever so long escalators in Heathrow!

Not having exchanged much in college, Ria went on talking about how Heathrow had been busy and the pilot had updated about the on-going cricket match while circling over the city. What an early morning ethereal spectacle it was beneath the aircraft. The series of red sloped roofs, Thames, embankment, like the architectural models one saw, then in scaled up real version in three dimensions and now in two dimensional prints in front of them. White framed windows behind the steel sculpture and the tree, corrugated metal decking roof blue, red brick, maple yellow leaves, trees green and yellow, the Thames, dark sky framing the trees in silhouette.

I wake up with a smile and know that smile is yours.

She wrote on the album and stacked it safely.

And there are some images we capture in our eyes by memorising. Sometimes we Photoshop them sepia or saturate them later, filter of Rosa Ingrid Bergman in full bloom with its resplendent colour in the centre. And couldn't be captured in any print was also the music in Covent Garden. Music binds the world. We are all a sea beneath, quite literally too. The music notation writing was taken up in Italian and practised worldwide in the same one language forever and ever.

One world and the journey in different metronome, in the hope of sun! Sumit went away to another country in the gulf and his call woke her up. "Good morning sweetheart!" "Good evening, my darling" the equally sleepy voice replied. Both wanted to slumber and dream a bit more. That lingered on the entire day for both and the people who breathed the same air. Love was simply beautiful. It gave you radiance, vigour in the heart, bloomed life as a fuel. A revelation of senses! And an awareness of a kind which otherwise would have just gone by. And at its behest everyone becomes a poet.

What elixir or Potion?

For the one drunk on life!

A vice could only be YOU

You

Till the vice is a vice

Not a necessity

For we sealed ourselves on each other

Did we bond forever

Or did we lose the tingling need, the want!

Did it feel any new?

It ran down deeper, since forever!

She was his window to the world of art and photography as he was to music and literature and technology and of a parallel galaxy out there to her. Sharing so, they would learn and meet half way. Computing, quantum physics and Tagore's poetry could be the topics of discussion in the same session of an evening spent together. A conscious trade off!

CHAPTER 7

Sharjah

The next teacher for the Pakka test was an extremely cautious one, constituted mainly of cold steel and non-malleable carbon. She tried to set Ria down at unease, any given opportunity. Or was that her natural disposition as an instructor! The native Filipino accent was quite dictatorially overlaid on the syntax of her English. She would point harshly at a slight mistake one could have made, pointing with a finger of her gloved hand.

The other day Ria asked to be picked for class from the Art area in Roulla, where she had walked down to see an exhibition. This was treated as a mistake by the ever-angry instructor, ranting about how on Fridays the drivers were ever so scared to be in that area and mimicked with a shaking of legs, supporting her dictum.

The cold snares continued and Ria kept on the wheel for the rest of the classes. Disapproving the quick manoeuvring of steering, Madame remarked how Ria must be handling things in life- not genteel' et al. But then she gave this student a minimum number of classes required, maybe because the ineligible student made her cross Roulla area a few times on pick-up or drop from the art area, much to the relief of both.

Sharjah being the cultural capital of the Arab world, the Heritage Museum area with the sweeping piazza and buildings that supported art, was of prominence. The narrow rectilinear streets cut at angles between the art buildings, leading to the stretch of Corniche that housed the market of spice, fishing hardware and the like, were interesting. Tourists were attracted to take a fill of the ambience and geniality of the place and to carry back bag full of merchandise.

The piazza's soothing hue of the earth-coloured finishes on the two-storeyed walls of the buildings in front, a tiny mosque and another bigger building punctuated with deep windows, replete with pavers, added dynamics to the angular streets. So did the ornate metal lighting fixtures.

Across the road of this piazza was the Sharjah Art Museum and above was the panoramic sky, escalating the scale of the open space and the sounds of random low chitter-chatter of the few visitors in the piazza, were pretty much all the sounds in the day. Added to these was azaan from the tiny mosque and the frequently flying airplanes leaving white streaks behind. And in the evening rattling of children's bicycles, if close by. This inviting treasure trove of architectural heritage abided to immediately exuding warmth and belongingness and the impression one took back was quite a lasting one. Ria liked to spend her days reading in the library of the Art Museum, as the beach had gotten hot.

Arrived then the day of Pakka test and Madame-de-Godzilla dropped Ria at the authorized building and remarked, "Go try if you can clear." The waiting room was brimming with ladies, prim prom and wearing easy smiles. As she entered, somebody said as-Salaam-Alaikum. Ria heartily replied and a few others retaliated to her greeting as well. All the ladies entered with a salutation. Of cheerful disposition, these tiny greetings added a congenial streak in the room, a fill of bonhomie.

An ambassador of teamwork, Ria was filled with an appreciation of the atmosphere. The ladies wore stunning makeup, especially on the eyes. The young girls had no makeup, their faces fresh and flawless. The black abayas were the common feature. A very young and vibrant girl asked her mom to call their driver and get her something to eat. Cookies were offered and she and Ria happened to chat. How Ria wished to capture her vibrancy and beauty on a roll but asking didn't feel appropriate.

Ria inquired if she was good with wearing abayas regularly. The young girl enthusiastically replied, "this is our traditional fashion "with a gleam in those eyes. Reinventing traditions for the contemporary lifestyle, the cut of burqas became more fashionably elegant and the buildings blended culture, history with the modern design, the Mashrabiyas were in glass-reinforced concrete, the traditional plaster in concrete and the graphics on the stationery and decorative items were of Pirates.

The examiner bade four of the females to sit in the car. Ria was to drive in second place. The first girl steered the car onto the main avenue. Once on this road, he asked her to drive faster, for the road was empty and it made no sense to drive that slow. Ria took on to the wheel on the same road and accelerated to a good speed.

Next, he instructed them to enter a locality. As pretty as a picture, the locality was full of trees in the gardens and empty roads, large plots and low height villas. It was here that Ria reduced speed and drove almost dead slow at the speed breaker before the T- junction, checked on the left side, manually as well before taking a right turn and zoomed again, once on the main avenue. She had been taught not to rely only on the left side mirror while overtaking or changing a lane to avoid the risk of a blind spot. One had to move head physically in front in order to check, going by the rules.

She drove quite a distance before she was asked to hand over the driving seat to the next girl. While she was in the colony, taking a turn, the inspector had spoken at length about something in Arabic. The places were switched twice again and then they waited in the same room with the earlier ease in the room gone. It started getting on to Ria too. She also started feeling that palpitation. The names were called at random.

Why was a mere license so important in this country, maybe because of the freedom associated with it. One of the girls who had accompanied her, walked towards her and remarked in English "you are surely done", for the instructor had commented" I hope all of you drive like her" Ugh and that was the moment and soon her name was called out too for getting the green. She was jubilant and again tried to make a fool of Sumit and again he fell for it and was eventually happy for his lady.

Aerosmith's Guns n Roses wasn't playing one evening on YouTube. The message said it was blocked. Blocked? It wasn't even porn, then why so? The search went on for a long time out of curiosity for much more. But the day had to be marked. Off they went to the Sahara Mall, her favourite one in the Emirate, for a quick celebration by sharing a cheesecake. Happiness was flimsy or plausible, depending on the perception and treatment.

She made a few good pictures in the art area, lucid in the morning and emery by the night. Tasveerein the other day were of people either in white or black ensembles with antique wrought iron lights adding to the majestic dull-coloured old charm in the alleyways and the garments imparting interesting movement in the urban draft. Two white Kandura clad men sat around a hookah. The huge area provided a choice of distance for the photographer. The sun wasn't down yet. The bricks in the courtyard were burnt out in the frame, nevertheless, it was compulsive to capture. It did make a tasveer.

Sheikh's daughter had undertaken command of rehabilitating and conservation of the heritage architecture in the entire emirate. And it was visible in the local Souq too, near the piazza.

Conforming to the environmental conditions and social values, the buildings were inward looking. The other buildings in the art area had a courtyard of immense proportion and rooms at the periphery. A huge installation of up-cycled material modified into abstract fluid forms, another one with them shaped into flowers on one wall. There were very few people around and each room was full of varied genres of ongoing artwork.

The other building had a small intimate courtyard, coloured birds in cages and cool, dark rooms. Painting was taught here in the evenings. The rooms were full of easels and paints and dummy heads, vases of all sizes and forms, innumerable supplies, a very cordial Egyptian teacher, and mostly head covered and not abaya-clad students. The atmosphere was very relaxed. She inquired about the fees and was taken aback by the answer, given the quality of the space. The government heftily supported the place.

Barjeels (the wind towers) in the buildings had always charmed and she stood admiring the sketches of the same displayed. The Iranian artist pompously explained them as Iranian influence on the architecture of UAE. And not only were they worn as elegant hats by the buildings above their roofs, they also played an important role in the natural air ventilation and cooling in a traditional way, the vents trapping and channelizing air into the shaft. And by regulating the direction of the incoming air, decrease the turbulence in the tower. As accentuated vertical elements visible in the background between traditional architecture and the modern, attention demanding buildings still further in the backdrop, Barjeels provided a remarkable transition.

With her tripod set afar, she shot the huge paved piazza lined by smooth mud-colour walls, punched by small square openings on the first floor. And still smaller square punches further at the top. The wooden bastions and the geometric parapets added some degree of decoration and interest to the otherwise plain and solid elevation, a reflection of the social and cultural values in the past. The response to the harsh natural environment and limited resources through innovative solutions was visible in the traditional architecture.

The organic pattern guided the buildings in close vicinity, in order to create narrow shaded alleys in the coastal city. Shade and sun factors created natural air movement. Low thermal conductivity was achieved through the use of mud mixture moulded into blocks, seashells in the lime mixture, plastered with chalk and water paste. Traditionally gypsum and coral stone were also used. Engaging information and the support to shoot pictures was extended eagerly by the shopkeepers to the tourists. Eyes not liking to get attracted to the cold colours, the areas of contrast needed to be identified, as light did not fall in a similar fashion. Taking images with the eyes was a simultaneous process, infused with passion. With naked eye you could focus wherever you wanted. Also, could focus on the reflection or through the glass. The camera behaved differently.

Over the weekend, the entire office team of Sumit's, along with their families, were invited for the desert party. The atmosphere was of cheer and good-natured rowdiness. It called for a show of candour, skin, cameras, kids, friendships that had grown beyond the office involving families, noise-happy people. The assembly point was Hatta. Land cruisers drove with some kind of attitude, hardly bothering about the pavements or any hindrances in their path.

At the gathering point, Ria had to get down quickly to buy herself a sunshade as her eyes squinted even at the slight hint of sunlight outside. These shades were tinted brown, an enhanced colour of the dunes ahead. With all the tyres deflated, the group mounted the machine camels again.

The caravan was handsome. Two families shared a cruiser. The south Indian young lady from the accompanying family in their land cruiser wanted a tiny break from the kid and was facilitated by the dad. He offered to sit with the kid while she sat in front but the kid implored her back. Ria was then encouraged to sit in the front seat since both the men had been to the desert safari before and the first timer's excitement level called for it. The buzz of the land cruiser steeply slipping into the slack without a predefined path was indeed action-packed. Theirs was amongst the first set of SUVs, followed by many in the trail.

With sand in the backdrop and afar, clouds of it behind the trail of the SUVS driving at all odd angles, indulged in the framing of the desert. Off white almost, rhythmic undulations of the dunes further away, in a wide expanse of view. Ria packed the camera away soon, meaning to come again in order to shoot.

The group assembled in the tents with much merrymaking and dance performances, in the middle of nowhere, by sunset. The drop in temperature was sudden. A flurry of activities in local entertainment was arranged in the tents. The compere made the ladies play a game with props to be stuck in the hair in a span of two minutes. Quite a spectre, ladies and children laughing at the straws jutting out of hair. So who cheated, asked the anchor. Amused looks and no one replied. The insistent anchor didn't give up, "you mean no one is honest enough to …"before he could complete, Ria got up "I did." "And the prize -a desert resort stay voucher goes out to this lady." Small pleasures and not a worry now about honesty at stake, the merry making continued.

With the license in hand she took the papers to the authorities for verifications "What? I am the one who would be learning, owning and driving the car"? She clarified.

"But you need a permission for that. Get these papers signed."

"Permission from whom? "She asked exasperated.

"From your husband."

"But I really don't need a permission from him in order to drive a car. With or without my husband or anybody inside."

"Well, in order to buy a car in this country you would need a written permission from him."

Why on earth did she have to ask him, in fact she was the one who had thought of it, applied, and learnt. Ria flanked down the innumerable steps of the Court building and composed herself and looked around. The court building with roof supported on two tall pillars at the entrance looked like a stable personality in white, wearing a gentleman's hat. The boats in front of the creek seemed similar to the ones seen from the roads in front of the Art area.

And lo, behold. This was the white court building she had seen from the other side of the creek and had spent quite a number of dirhams to reach in a taxi. When were the Dubai taxis going to be introduced here, in the low profiled brother emirate.

She took pictures of the bay of ships in front of the art area, now from the other side of the creek and so far by road.

The papers were in Arabic. In the evening, over a glass of cranberry juice, sprawled on the wide red leather sofa's hand rest – listening to "Naam Sabah likhna," the song with a beautiful rendition about lost love in Kashmir, Sumit signed those papers for a car that she would be buying with his money and driving to explore the country and have a gala time, again with his money. They joked about it and over the permission papers signed and hearty laughter, called it a day.

Sumit had shortlisted two Toyota cars and they went to the showroom, selected one in half an hour and got it in a week's time. This is how the government takes taxes here, said the manager, going over the elaborate paperwork and charging for stuff unknown. The car gave wings to Ria. This country had gained its freedom from British rule only in 1971; the development had been tremendously swift and in quite a planned manner, especially with the infrastructure. The roads were safe, wide, lit, planned and inviting. Unhindered avenues and the thrill of speed! Unknown roads led her to new experiences. People were playing with mean machines and with racing camels.

Along with the car came the freedom of venturing far everyday. She hoped to explore the sand safari as well again with Sumit, but that wasn't his idea of a weekend. He wanted to join a high-end club for recreation, to spend his weekend.

Nevertheless, it wasn't a deterrent, only the limits were to be respected. And the country was safe. The camels had a right of way. The camera, mostly by the road side or a little higher on a sturdy stand, made up for stunning pictures of the unblemished horizon, dull golden sand of Sharjah and creamy sands towards Ajman. The patterns in the sand, solitude of the desert and sometimes thrill of quad bikes and jeeps trying to conquer the challenging dunes made for great shots. The pictures of desertscape!

The architecture of downtown Dubai was a loud statement, fluid and art noveau, extremely exciting. Another kind of a loud statement. Of facadicism and vanity. About one third or more of the height at top was unused and vied by one after the other, a still taller skyscraper. But with the camera in hand, it was more a mysterious world, full of boxes, shapes, angles behaving playful with the sun, sky, people, luminance and with each other. Through her lens, the uniqueness of their elemental forms and sometimes, spatial context was fascinating. The distinguishing of these, the process of capturing the nuances was like extracting the form of art, from the field that always fascinated her and known as mother of all arts.

As a built subject, the unique character of the build up and the environment had to be captured creatively. Following the light movement at particular angles and with the prerogative of few edits to refine them. For the vertical lines to be the leading lines in order to retain perspectives, corrective lines and lenses and the wait for the blue hour took her to over bridges far off. The traffic, sandstorm and people were situational while shadows related to the time of the shoot. It was as vital to document these just as one dealt with documenting the heritage assets. And so, she did.

The daily newspaper in print was interesting. It spoke about new developments on the front page and usually carried a picture of the Sheikh of Dubai going about his daily affairs. The fourth estate seemed responsible in covering various facets of positivity. The other day there was a picture of Sheikh Mohammed bin Rashid Al-Maktoum in a chic suit and without the traditional headgear, besides the Queen, a debonair. Ria's eyes zoomed in and out, she took it to Sumit who was dashing through the door for office, to take a glimpse and he too held a smile of amused admiration on his way out.

The stringent laws reduced the crimes or maybe they were held by the fourth estate. Whichever way, the newspaper every morning held optimism and interest. On the volte face watching news of India and fretting over the state of affairs was tolling. Once they called a friend in Jaipur after hearing about a bomb blast in the news, he didn't sound as troubled as the couple in Sharjah. By and by the couple stopped watching news from India as a matter of routine, so as not to go into a tirade over it.

On Fridays, if you left the water gallons outside along with the coins required to replenish it, the bell just did not ring at all. The water gallons were exchanged, money never lost. Seldom beggars rang the bell and you refused them once and that was it.

Poornima, a socialite and an acquaintance through a cousin, offered Ria to get introduced to a get-together group. But Ria had so much to explore in the new country by herself that she had no time or inkling for socializing. As the camera drew closer to the conducive Sheikh Zayad Road, the spine between skyscrapers, breathing the air, the people, the culture, the avenues and inhaling the essence, it was well consumed.

She started enquiring about the possibility of a part time job. Part time job seemed out of question in the working ways of Sharjah. Also, she started checking out the photography exhibitions. The exhibits were images of the deserts, the falcon and the man and camels alike in the magnanimous desert. The desert was a photographer's heaven by itself and she decided to go further in the interiors. Mr Negi's yoga classes for stabilizing hands came handy here. Sandstorms were one thing the camera was scared of and had to be protected from.

On the roadside by the Burj Khujjam round about, en-route Sumit's office sitting outside on large cushions on the floor were musicians playing to the passer by to commemorate the celebration indoors. It was a three-day evening affair and he got a video of the same to show. That became the subject of Ria's shoots for the next two evenings.

As the car's distance of travel increased, the road to Abu Dhabi offered great vistas and Al-Ain's low-lying valley brought night photography opportunities. From a distance on the way back, Sumit pointed out the zig-zag trail of the lights in the distant hills leading to a bigger one at the helm, the beaming moon. The enchanting full moon! Where else did the moon look like that? It was a long exposure picture and the couple duly waited by the hard shoulder.

She spoke to a few colleagues of Sumit, who opined there was no prevalent concept of part time working. She pursued with all the firms she could lay her eyes on, visiting and dropping resume as per the listing. And in the process of interviews, negotiating on the number of hours. There was plenty still to explore and learn and do and then there was the sea by night. How could she miss out on that with a full-time job.

In the Mubarak centre, before she could give it up, having tried all across the emirate, the receptionist of an office on the fifth floor, ushered her in to meet the proprietor. As chance would have it, in the same building, the last person to interview her had refused the job because Sumit wasn't ready to let the employer keep her passport.

Mr Sabah on the fifth floor was an old man with a milky soft complexion, receding white shiny soft hair and a gentleman's smile. He stood up to greet Ria with a friendly handshake. His fragile and soft hands had the same warmth and candour as of her own. Ria was hired after a conversation of fifty minutes and was shown around the office. She wasn't asked to submit the passport nor was required to change the sponsorship or comply with any such formality.

First day in Sabah's office, she reached by car and parked it behind the complex in the kachcha parking. The time walking and by car was the same.

The office had two large rooms, two office cabins, a studio and a processing workshop. And there was an eight-pax conference room where Ria spent her day. The pictures on walls shot from high altitudes were surreal, of buildings piercing through clouds. Those of fog receding between buildings and showing off the skyscrapers a level above. Strings of lights on the road about to go off, getting the city ready for the day. And of the Etisalat building with its signature sphere.

In the afternoon she returned to her car being blocked by another one in the huge ground behind Mubarak centre and the sun was burning everything down. A passerby suggested calling the police. Salutation in Arabic was heard from the other side of phone connection and she answered in English. Finally, the conversation settled in Urdu and Hindi respectively. In a span of five minutes the police got into the records of the other driver from the number plate, took him on call and the driver was there.

She went through a lot of documented work in the conference room for the next few days. Sabah wanted her to acclimatize with the country, geography and specially the local ethics and work culture. Arabic coffee, art cafes, spatial impression, ethereal shifting sands into infrastructure, he had witnessed it all. And aerial images of Dubai and Abu Dhabi from yesteryears with as many buildings as you could count on fingers.

And there were the impressive pictures he had created out of road signage and graphical content on the ground. One stark black and white was of the Jebel Hafeet road, signage of camels having a right of way, the dark tar of the road, zebra markings and calves crossing it. The order created by ochre and the golden sand getting richer in colour and contrast by the late afternoon sun, the time for long shadows. She looked for something to set a sense of scale in the expanse of the desertscapes. Camels usually were the models for that.

She made a mental note of going there over the weekend.

The studio worked from 8:00 to 13:00 and 16:30 to 19:30. The afternoon was for siesta and off went the entire staff home to return in the evening. The mornings in the office were eventful. The cool vibe of a colleague's congeniality, the pleasantness of reaching a workplace and a promising day ahead! The tone was set by the pleasantly familiar face of Abraham and the occupied, purposeful look on George's face. He was the one going out for approvals, that being mostly the concern in this country rather the budget. Ria walked into their room first with greetings, warming up chitter chatter, then to her workstation, a recent addition in the conference room.

George and Abrahim had been there for 17 devoted years and carried the massive work on their shoulders. There was a minimum number of employees' regulation from the government. Domelvo was a tall man of robust built from Africa who, in spite of being allocated a whole room to him, was the loudest and often from his room came voices of arguments with visitors. Also in George and Abraham's room sat Zia, the Pakistani boy who handled the creative writing. The boss a Pakistani, the partner an Arab and receptionist from Philippines, the office was an example of inter-continental integration.

The Arbab was an odd greedy man, unlike most of them as George explained, who would negotiate off-hand arrangement of share percentage and not meddle in the work or worked together and added value. The Arbab was fond of restraining and intervening every now and then. He was also very fond of bringing fruits from his estate on his visits. Ria was introduced to him and he offered a pungent smelling fruit. As she politely declined, she sensed glances from people standing behind the Arbab and complied. That Saturday she returned home with a huge watermelon to an amused Sumit receiving her at the door, one of the many that Arbab had got along with a variety of fruits in huge packaging.

Ria hung the print of the image she had recently captured. A harmony. Like the colour of water depending on the suspended or dissolved solids, reflecting from the sky or surrounding materials, more than the water itself.

Sabah was a subject master in studio photography like Abhiyansh. Besides the light, your own vision could make a picture spectacular or terrible. Pictures are created not clicked. " Tasveer" in Urdu again was one of the words he spoke with a phenomenal passion. His use of side illumination from openings in the buildings for portraits during sunrise and sunset was marvellous, the dramatic application enhanced the texture and form of the picture dramatically.

Sabah was of the view that ample of drama available in natural lighting's reflection off surfaces was to be used instead of enhancing it with other light sources. His prominent work was in black and white, which he described as unapologetically simple. The b/w portraits in which shade and light plays the dance sequel to the tones.

His knack of using layering with the natural light itself rendered the work impressionably. Especially with the series he did on porches and verandas of Pakistan.

Now she began to interpret the deeply profound influence Abhiyansh had had on her work and vision. Watching Sabah's ability to concentrate on the music and cut out the noise in a tasveer, Abhiyansh's phrases also started ringing in her head. Instinct kicks. Whatever you want to be noticed, positioned thus in light. You could hold the viewer's gaze thus in your entire composition. Uneven light, dappled shadows were unflattering. It all struck her as she started executing projects of similar nature.

Of the words floating and dancing in the air sans a wall, in and out

The whirl is not of the words, my dear.

Of the essence!

For we know and interpret different languages

At the enchanting time of setting sun, the house had a flowing space to sit in between the indoor and the outdoors, unusual to the design practice in this region.

Sabah guided her through the villa shoot. Long distance view is what draws people and villa plots were standard throughout. A big nice garden or an offset available for the same! Pedestrian views which are reinforcing and narrow beams that would build beautiful colours. He trained her with layered lighting and attentive details highlighting. Cooler colours to soothe the eye from the harsh sun. Mustard incandescent, the soft light for barely a glow effect and how to make use of the glare, he highlighted. He made her practice fill-in-flash, which she couldn't master earlier. And also made her master the digital post-processing.

The streetscape possessed amazing subtlety- the form of the roundabout and the colours blended with the street and the sands far away. Lighting conditions and character of the material gave a visual language specific to the building. The ribbed walls punctuated with dark glass and the use of not too many kinds of materials gave them more of a monolithic effect. Softly walking towards the lit tree, he elaborated about trees as light features – light bouncing back from leaves. Integrating light into architectural features- like up lighting colonnade, warm hue of block - the modest brick that has been around forever, unlike the pretentious glass and granite.

A new domical structure appeared on her way to a project in Dubai. She made a note to capture the same in the morning twilight and harsh afternoon light too. The design objective of the buildings seemed to be the same, to make a bold statement.

You wanted to begin anew, the country offered more than that.

Away from the humdrum, competition of peers, it was all right to be doing what they wanted. There was no social pressure. Now a routine of work and exploration formed. The balance as experienced- no less, no more.

The rain caused all those sensations, wet and wild! He didn't want to substitute the silence of love making with words. Fiddler for words that she was, not understanding the symphony the touch of their fingers was producing, the only way to stop her was to seal her hungry luscious lips and keep them locked in engagement while moving on with the rest of sensations.

Wondering how people were indoors on a rainy Saturday. Wasn't the downpour supposed to force one outside, to dance or run and sing or just stand? She took onto the wheel and throughout Sumit worried about the wading car on the water-logged roads and didn't enjoy a wink. When he caught his breath, once back to Corniche, they agreed on watching the spectacle from the veranda of Qanat next time.

Well, the next spell of rain didn't oblige anytime soon but they did go to sit in Qanat over sumptuous food and walked towards the end of the corridor. There seemed to be some activities further down, a fair uncelebrated entrance to the hall, which was a flower land. Flowers were strewn everywhere, exquisite floral arrangements on the tables and many more in the making. Reeking of equally magical an aroma. A mesmerising fervour! The flower show was opening the next day. Didn't it have the same hustling wonder as the Kinari bazaar's charm in Chandni Chowk after the slight evening drizzle!

She asked permission for shooting the other side of the 'blue bay' as she called it- this side selling dry fruits selling by kilos similar to the gold sold in Dubai. The creek had been cut to bring water in and add to the length of the coastline substantially by landfill; the land was reclaimed thus at various locations throughout the country. Sir asked her to leave the camera behind and walk through the entire length first, talking to people or inhaling the surroundings or all of it or may be observing something beyond her comprehension.

He added that the area had also seen progression and slow evolution. Emotional impact and moment, both she could highlight in her work there and he discussed and explained in detail about the philosophy applicable. Always the one adding to the conversation with an open mind, she could recall strange phrases Abhiyansh quoted but never elaborated on.

He welcomed her suggestion of shooting the area. We all have to work the same in life, but ambition in a man makes him so charming. Some of us choose what we work on, what to do ourselves, and what to get done, he said. Few of us work up our minds. The people we think are not working are actually sometimes working up their minds only, seldom in a productive way. They are worse off than those who actually work and tire. Its the best to do what you really want to do and like to do, for we will always find means to get it done. Perception from the image, as much as she could produce and what was felt being there while on shoot, was to be captured. Reflecting thus, the camera and Ria walked off to the creek together, doing what they wanted to do, even if to sit together in the nothingness.

She presented her assignment on the lines of a viewpoint of the 'romance of a far away city' as she had done with Shahjahanabad in Delhi. Her idea was bringing those images to people who might not in their lifetimes visit those places. So, the visuals had to be true, contextual and history was important. After thorough research of the places, the time, context, and connection were established. The relationship with the people, surroundings, the impact of it as a part of the location of space! And architecture being able to motivate a link with the community.

Frames reflected in the tasveerein and her notes on civic sense, aesthetic and function she brought to office in a week. Sabah said if he could, he would go back in time and click the impact and the story of the evolvement with her as he himself enjoyed documenting real time projects in the present. They would become history later.

A series she was assigned to, for enhancing the skill of applying layered lighting again, shooting retail facades in the malls. She carried her flowing dress in a bag along. After the shoot, she changed, wore her hair in a neat bun and came out with a surprising gait. Sumit kept looking as she walked towards him, the amused smile appeared on his face and he looked sideways. She came and sat in front of him. Against hope he didn't react, as anticipated but the sly smile kept giving away his happiness and the expression of what now? The security guy came running to the music not having stopped at the call for prayer. That broke off the reverie and as Ria had hoped, they did go to the Burj -Al -Arab.

Thursdays called in for a very early weekend. Friday morning outings were sacrosanct. The two of them would look forward to the entire week to visit a mall and share a Cinnabon roll. Four forks and knives dug in the middle of the creamy sin, tackling each other and the sinful food would disappear in a jiffy. Pictures from these trips would be then discussed in the evening and again the camera and the zealous couple were ready for the next day's evening outing.

At the parking lot in Sahara mall, while reversing her car, a lady hit her stationery car. The two ladies waited patiently for the cop. The cop discussed with the localite at length in Arabic and asked Ria to come to the nearest police station. Ria put her foot down and demanded for a green slip. They spoke again in Arabic and requested her yet again to accompany to the police station. Whatever the setting was, Ria remained stern. The cop complied and Ria did get the green slip without further ado.

Now that Ria joined a job, Sumit took to a volte-face, suggesting that since she had gone out, met people and carried on with her work, so she must have nice things to add in their evening conversations. Again instigated, she would rhapsodize about what was going by, her interpretation of everyday things, Sabah and so on. The value of input was the same, the context changed and the evenings flew by.

What were they doing, sending money home, building assets there, but living here in a foreign land and there was sometimes a pang for near and dear ones. Sometimes, for the monsoon and for thick quilts in December. What was it that they were lacking in India?

Recalling geography, India was resourceful in flora, minerals. The civilisation was rich historically and embedded with endless feats. If holding the media, doctoring it was such a crime, what must it be which the leaders (monarchy or not) must be doing right so that it did feel peaceful and safe here in reality? Why couldn't the citizens' value for life be enhanced back home?

The systems were definitely not in place and the execution of policies left to chance, more than arrangement. Much of the valuable time was lost in arguments and in 'what could have been'. And the people in power, long gone off in history, were not allowed to resign still, by the current sessions of the Parliament. And as the German artist said, our repute for corruption was world famous. Why was there so much of mud flinging and distrust? Whose perpetual benefit was it to always bring up controversies?

And so much so, why not use history for important lessons learnt in the right and defined interests, and not for mulching endless controversies?

CHAPTER 8

Artist

"The past is not past, it is still passing by"

-Octavio Paz, Mexican poet

I collected the moments... as pearls

Abhiyansh: She was as mad and restless as me.

Ria: He was also the sturdy balanced guy, been there done that kind, now settled.

Abhiyansh:

In the mountains...

"The oneness in nature's realm sensed as an enthralling experience"

Later when you lie down on your back and see, you were only a small speck in the universal picture of consummation.

"Need you with me, to feel complete, to look into the sky". This "you" was muddled. Muddled!

One look at her face, Aica's face and that in itself was an eternity. Her movement was like a part of a symphony. Odette in Swan lake's free flow of the art form. Ballerina with coherence and grace, fragile as the look of net and lace she wore... He distracted himself from thinking further.

Ria:

That insightfulness and vividness of dreams – were plenty, of what one could care for. And when awake, there was ample stuff to think about and see, write and read, draw and click and eventually blend it all! My dreams were panoramically detailed. Write stories with your camera, sing to yourself- Just be!

To be ordinary yet be in harmony!

The Excursion Together to the Hills:

The criss-cross lines of the electric supply, transformers against the green fields in the distance and ten minutes out of the metro madness, one started appreciating the beauty of the farms. And in one of these fields, the team would have shot the famous' rain in field' picture. Rain drops in a slant, captured as lines as offsets, farmer family taking charge in the rain, and the green fields with the entire frame, clearly in focus. What would have been the settings, Ria tried to calculate the depth of field and dozed off.

The equipment was all neatly packed. The safari was smooth. She slept in the back seat with all her lighting equipment. Her regret of damaging his fisheye lens in the rain last monsoon came up.

Abhiyansh:

She had paid through her nose and listened to the sermons with a bowed head. Her apology and regret in the eyes were genuine as her co-relation to casualty was low. That had left me confused. If that was so, how could she recklessly jump into the rain without bothering about the protocol of lens under the tree and an umbrella if not under the designated hood? Money could buy the lens and it would be fine in time.

We took a break before reaching the resort. This girl, who had been dozing all through the journey with her green tinted shades still on, was seen running down the hills, both arms flying. Even Negi for once stood watching with interest, leaning by the jeep. For a minute, he said "let us forget work today" aloud, finding himself immersed in the flow of an energetic show. Though the words remained floating in the air, ready to rest somewhere as he continued witnessing her speedy rendition of the run, they couldn't rest anywhere. No one elaborated, knowing too well the assignment had to continue, as it always did.

I would have got offended if Negi had brought up any comparison between the two, Aica and Ria. He was smoking and I stood next to him. Signalled a no with my hand, as he held his smoke out for me, inhaled the air and let out a long sigh. I prided myself in the ability to quit anything and declined the offer. Negi carried on and we kept staring into the distance in absolute silence. The comradeship had stood the test of time.

But with those words still afloat, I mounted in my trekking shoes and set a path to walk the hills too.

Ria:

So why don't you go and count the deciduous trees in the neighbourhood?

Stupid as it sounded, Abhiyansh left the team in exasperation. The team sent a day back hadn't lived up to his expectations in the pre-shoot set-up.

Abhiyansh:

Neither was I in the mood nor I was so clumsy to give heed to that. Something more ludicrous, I had never heard.

I walked away from the scene. How could I stand my people working like that! Just lifted my backpack of 30 Kg, shoved it under the tent and walked away.

The long leaps and then normal breathing at intervals soon converted into ambling. A yellow butterfly came fluttering from somewhere and before an understanding or acknowledgement, touched my left cheek and turned away, in the same quick fluttering speed. That tiniest of a fluttering touch somehow renewed my consonance and I resumed my pace. Before the tent came back to my sight, I had counted more of evergreen than the deciduous trees.

At the sight of the tent, I wildly hoped that the work was done. Everything was just as is, the way I had left, and even the props were at the same position. But my mind was pellucid and I looked at stuff from a fresh perspective. Not having had taken a break in a long while, being overworked was much against my regular working style. I processed the preceding last few days; viewed targets in regained perspectives and formulated the action plan. And vowed to take a long break post this shoot.

*****

The resort to be photographed was on a steep, contoured site. There was a spread of cottages with a sharp gradient in their roofs. Most of the cottages had stilt seating and an attic living room, both the areas glowing warmly in the evening. The light lux of the stilt was lower than of the attic, which could have been intentional, providing the focus from outside as per the lighting designer, if there was one on the design panel. Also, the coloured slopes and contours, if the built up's colour was considered neutral, would impart a spectacle of shades. The site had to be photographed in the twilight and in the night the next evening, so the preparation had to be carried right away and the site studied. Ria was to assist with the dawn photography.

Lighting needed evaluation. Small windows in the faraway bits and pieces were identified. In the hills, near and remarkably distant, featured an abundance of coloured squares and rectangles, without your control of switching them off. Whether or not they gelled with your story of immediate visuals, they had to be reckoned with.

Abhiyansh treaded along the contours of the site, absorbing all the details. The positioning for their strategic inconspicuous placement was to be determined. The LED sources he had carried for strategic placement were being handled by Mr Negi as a part of the logistics. The final approvals came from Abhiyansh but Negi could visualize and work out nuances and mostly they were in tandem. That calculative mind of Negi with a pre-emptive approach could understand the heightened artistic bent of Abhiyansh's mind which was beyond the comprehension of most. Maybe, all that Negi perceived as out of ordinary or deranged, he attributed to Abhiyansh and that worked. Also, he was Abhiyansh's Hermano, safeguarding his creative vision since he was prone to adulation by muses and patrons alike.

Negi knew a platonic relationship was the fodder for Abhiyansh. He survived on it but wasn't delusional.

*****

Abhiyansh:

My day started being refreshed every morning and ready to take whatever the day had to offer. The schedules for shoots were fixed once a week between Negi and me. Besides that, my time had a command over me and vice versa. And to convert whatever was at hand into work. A permanent relationship with any inspiration wasn't my forte.

Do not know too much. Do not find too much, he said to his young friends. For when you do that –you lose the charm of not knowing it all. Even when you know how much nicer it was, it was non-retractable. The youngsters would shrug this off.

Life has its own way of teaching. Only the mind had to be kept open. It even teaches to make out between right and wrong. Somebody's right could be your wrong if it was all subjective and cleared when one actually decided to look.

Ria:

Happy in awareness of the early morning hill's beguiling hues, perfect for waking up, I picked up my jacket from the tanned leather sofa, which was a prop. It was a long day, much to look forward to. We were also to prepare for the fashion shoot scheduled the next day. I delayed myself, sloppily checking around. Then opened the tent and stretched, looking at the distant mountains and the tent, both in the same profile.

Yoga postures at a neighbouring tent inspired me. Later I see a picture of me doing an asana looking towards the hills. Didn't know how many people were awake before me and working in the dark. I was captured in a frame with thatched roofed cottages on the podium in the left and green coloured cross poles, lanterns hanging down and a bird perched on the top left.

*****

To emphasize the horizontal, the resort did not overpower the landscape. Abhiyansh admired the kind of architecture where the segregation of spaces became blurred. It merged with the plantation, with the hill as the backdrop. Here in the hills, he also admired how the designer had articulated tiny, contained spaces like blobs, if you were to see from a distant drone. The transitory spaces, the stilts had been dealt with in a contained, sophisticated fashion. Seating, a hearth and a mini shelter from the wrath of weather.

The entry experience of the block was bold, to the eye and of warm interiors, once inside. Like that impressive handshake, which leaves you with a good impression of the receiver. The movement in spaces was splendidly free and inviting between the exterior and the interiors. Inside the singly loaded corridor, was another block, in the mound that led to the rooms, creating a sense of anticipation as the visitor moved through it. From the dark corridor, as you moved into the foyer, the lit lounge created a sharp contrast. The bay windows with earthy finishes and ample cosy cushions were a haven for a book reader. The bed looked into the distant dark sky, into the stars unknown and the feeling of anticipation, which such spaces create. The cluster of three units each was staggered and connected through a lounge. Tall hedges separated the individual units and each unit had a tent in front, for night-time opportunities. The twilight with the tents lit up and the lanterns forming intricate patterns enhanced the flavour of the marvellous architecture.

Where the contours were steep, the long deck at the entrance level extended without the railing, the roof of the suite below, the mumty steeply inclined and opening to the view of the valley and it was a slightly inclined cuboidal mass. And the thin, lithe tall trees piercing through the volumes were a spectre.

Vernacular construction methods used by local masons with the knowledge and practice of the art was undertaken, the owner emphasised. The women folk were given a facility for local handicrafts and other measures were taken into consideration to minimize the harm to the environment and the effect on local balance sociologically. It was a quotable work well done and responsibility adhered to, in all aspects.

Abhiyansh's gadgets were scratch less. He took a long time setting them up, small aperture and long exposure. Even if he could do that in a jiffy. Night photography was to be undertaken at unique angles and light reflections. The noticeable light source that night was the neon sign from a far-off shop.

He held a remote for exposure of 20 seconds, to avoid blur. The road was being sprayed for the night photography. Reflections of glistening features, lights, internal reflections in puddles were the effect to be explored and generated.

Ria took multiple shots of the artist at work in the lobby, left hand supporting her chin. She wore full sleeves with unbuttoned cuffs and her pencil at work on a pile of papers. This same image was given to her ten days later as a farewell gift.

Next day, as he warmed up to the camera, the shoot was ready. She was asked to handle flexi to reflect light as desired by the photographer. Abhiyansh was speaking to the model. He had specified a pin up in the dress, which he wasn't satisfied with. He also spoke about the energy, comfortable look and intricacies of what he wanted. He kept two of the models engaged in conversation, bringing the vivaciousness in the image. One was a lady in forties whose face spoke of calmness and a nimble look with the salt and pepper hair of hers.

Documented was his work in office, depicting an awareness of déshabillé. And also, there was work where the lack of it was the catalyst in its metamorphosis into unblushing art. The latter one was not with professional models. It was with portraits of phenomenal women as a point of view of themselves in the frame and for their own record. A connection. His complete connection! Each a narrative of beauty in a silent and unpretentious point of view. Abhiyansh's forte was getting close to that POV of his women. His viewers, he said, could respond to the former art with a thrill. The latter one could create awe or calm the spirit, either way. He was pretty concerned about the viewers. Enamoured viewers interested him too. So did the critics. But curious questions about them didn't bring straight answers. Respect for his subjects strictly prevented him for commenting on their stories.

Multitude of shots, there was nothing he was not taking care of. It was as if he was bringing out the persona of the two ladies. This one was for an aunt and niece depictive shot. He spoke to the elder lady constantly about her kith and kin till he could catch the right emotional expression in her face. Dealing reverently, the frame he created exuded an aura of a relationship.

Next, he went on to clicking the younger model in a different format. The props quickly changed and the model lay down on the slope, resting on the prop. There was a lot of formality now about the ambience with an acquired expression, the product and the scene set up. Even the long necklace she wore did not fall at its own accord. He seemed to be designing each and every centimetre of the result that would be for best detail and tonal shading.

The shaded spaces under canopies were shaped as inverted tuberoses, with rimmed in off-whites.

Motion pictures with slow shutter speed- 1/15 made sense. He called Ria over and described how it should have been at a slow shutter speed – say 1/ 15.

To explain the 1/ 15th to her was a nightmare.

Post the shoot, models had all returned and the crew took the day off. The trek led to a waterfall and a valley beyond. Unexpected that it was, people ran the last leg. Ria had sat on a rock, leaning her head on the next bigger one, feet resting on tiny ones, gazing at the valley and the waterfall.

The rocky flow. A picture of hers, caught unawares, was gifted to her by the office as a farewell gift later. Of the loveliest green moss and white surfed water, blissfully at peace with herself and her natural smile. In her pursuit to find spirituality, love or whatever higher force, it had led to the find. A halt at the waterfall, looking at this serene river, listening to the music, the stunning mildly green and the white surf gushing through the rocks singing all to itself, loud enough not to be distracted by any other noise. How the river flows continuously, largely by itself.

YOU

For whenever I find myself, I find YOU too

The sojourn of the shaded rocks, the music of the river and the dancing shadows of the trees..

the slight shower of the misty flow in the air.

For when WE are in communion, when YOU are a part of me, why do I need to find myself

My skin feels pleasant against your rock, your hills make me look up, your wind makes my strands fly and I feel pulled...

Harmony is here.

Why do I need to go back?

Just let me be.

For again YOU will need to embrace me with your winds

Well, you did give me this body to look after.

Okay, will go, send me.

She had sat there for a long-time witnessing people enjoying and waving to her to come over to the falling water, of her surroundings, magnanimous on each side. She couldn't budge from where she sat. So strong was the sense of completeness in her own positioning in the entire scene and ruminating over the picture, it rejuvenated her.

All is fulfilled and happy. It's a perfect world. We get what we ask for, when the girl in the mirror is happy and we are right and fearless.

This farewell gift along with a fish eye lens in hand, she readied herself for whatever came next.

Ria:

For when I smile, I see you smiling.

As if, that one is my face and when I use those muscles, you smile. Or is it me.

And it didn't rain, which was good.

For the eyes had no time and the feet would run past the puddle. Some trees, like the dok-phut, did not need coloured petals to glorify them. And neither did one need a downpour. Leaves, shedding themselves, were good enough.

*****

She couldn't be bound. It was the passion that oozed out of her, in her actions and even in her arguments about work. That passion interested him the most.

She was promptly called back for another assignment as a freelancer. Passionate pictures and the people, who would click them, would be available without hunting. But the epitome of live passion's electrification of the air in his studio had now become a compulsion.

Abhiyansh:

The rain falling in the ebony! Getting stronger and drumming harder as it gets still darker.

The rain brought her fragrance back to me. The monsoon was common at the places, hers, and mine. The water splashing on me must have touched her too.

We are a unique kind, had to meet. And reinvent!

We could! We might!

Love is definitely a conscious decision of the soul.

*****

The weather caught up with her better side, like a gardener and nature's relationship. The work was identified to engage her.

The refusals of taking up projects in constant continuation were genuine because life interested her.

Selected work then that he was sure, she would not say no to!

Ria hadn't seen this melancholic and furtive work of his earlier. It was related to Aica. That endearing lady could be a reason for silent rebellion against the business of easy living and could lead to poignant work? It was unbelievable.

To reciprocate, love accepted was equally important. When a force is leading something towards you, the reaction has to be of acceptance or an equal force from you too. Like when you really really crave, the craving itself becomes appealing. Unrequited craving could be more powerful. We all change with time. The people close to us also bring about that change.

Post that experience, again he had tried lesser to think and more to feel. Pain as a fuel had led to his valued superlative work, which, if taken further, could have started carrying morbid hints to it.

People wish for each other in heaven. In hell they wish for themselves. Heaven and hell, my dear friend is here. In this very life!

Abhiyansh:

I AM- my whole world.

And a little lost

The wall was there, would be in my studio for as long as the studio existed. How I wished...

Muse was a free soaring soul. You couldn't fasten her; only enjoy watching her in flight, while she was in range.

When she pierced into your soul with her gaze, it was difficult to hold yourself. All that I wanted around her was that she didn't look into my eyes. My effect on her and not of hers on me!

Ria:

Like the endlessly synchronised movements of a ballerina, achieved through relentless practise. And his images justifying, actually celebrating the same. Many of the images were also from the dressing rooms. Also were the images of fury and disasters. And of complications unbound.

Abhiyansh in "We":

We had played sonata and not a full symphony together. When you attain bliss, you do not give a damn about what you wanted to do in order to attain it.

The white room with mirrors might teach Aica some shying.

"Ask mirrors in the white bedroom "he said.

He did not look at the photographs of these muses, only at the fragments in his mind. And at fullness of the soul!

Capturing it was a part of feeling it. As much as you can capture the essence of that feeling in a shot, the successful endeavour of the photographer comes out in the picture.

The livid greens, the stone, the purple leaves beaming out of the turf, the one and half a feet of red sandstone steps besides the brick structure without the balusters, her luminous face against it, his frame had suddenly become miffed. In his realm of the etheric setting the spontaneity had disappeared. His heart did not beam, the pictures now felt lifeless. Letting go was painful.

Maybe he loved with intensity, without restraint. He surely clicked pictures with the same passion. The ladies had all gone away but the pictures stayed, archived.

About her:

It was such a bliss to be ordinary, to breathe and love. Aica always felt pity for the celebrities and the high profiled, requiring them to carry on with formality. She could hug a stranger on the road; hold hands with a client or a subject of his pictures, in consideration. She could actually listen to herself and "just do."

Moreover, her being lithe and agile in movement, people naturally got a sense of a cub passing by. And she thought she subtly glided by. And if she suddenly spurred into action, she became irresistible, even felt edible to the men with exquisite taste. Spring in her feet, by the time you stood still to catch her, she was a whiff in the air, killing the next set of people.

Ria's looks were pleasant, North Indian sharp features. It was the material under the skin, which was mind blowing and altogether put, simply beautiful.

CHAPTER 9

Sabah-ud-din-Siddiqui

Sabah walked back towards his room after the afternoon Namaaz, passing by the conference room. He was a manifestation of faith himself, face shining, slow movements, courteous gestures, and kind demeanour.

Faith in time. Time, that is Now!

Vast or minor, history is important to be preserved, he said. And equally important was to date it precisely. No wonder he was reflecting the thoughts of the monarch; Burj across the country had been restored with success.

The pictures Sabah had shot from his haveli in Pakistan depicted a proportionate scale along with an efficient use of space. He said his only brief to the designer was to use space like how a cobbler does while cutting out the sole. Even though he was sure of not returning to Pakistan, he built his haveli there with gusto.

Documenting the conservation projects of Sharjah and Ajman constantly occupied the office. Building photography was his forte and he had progressed parallel to the economy of the country, bagging prestigious projects one after the other. While documenting the extension of cultural projects, he had himself seen to the right choice of stone, chandan wood, landscape plants and their procurement from foreign lands. That had led to a friendship with the Sheikh of Ajman and he proudly displayed six images of the two together in a warm handshake. And another one was of them sitting together for iftaar. The documentation and its importance were something he had learned from the British.

Establishing connection was Sabah's strong suit. Achieving desired gestures through an understanding of body language was Abhiyansh's. Ria pondered over these and strove to assimilate both the styles in her work. In working with them, both had given her the pace to match her own metronome, to excel.

Sabah had clicked photographs of cities around the world. He had captured the vernacular, the inherent heart of the cities, pictures of the construction, buildings and the people involved in construction/ structural systems fascinated him and he had a collection of "in the making" from the places he visited. People in relation to the building were so important; both didn't exist without the other. The same he had sketched and painted too, in his youth.

The behaviour and tenor of a countryman, in relation to that of the development, were also a part of his work. The motion trail images of people and landscape, as if caught in a movement, in passing by, signifying a visual memory one would make from his car trip across continents. The visual thrill of a deep blue window making its way out from the stonewall, some outgrowth of moss and a creeper with white flowers. Paved stone, in front. The same frame behaved differently, the cobalt blue window as a subject gave way to another subject in a few hours when a lady peeped out, her head tilted and hands rested on the sill. The deepest of the Prussian blues in the sky, with a luminous full moon providing a backdrop against the sharp edges of buildings, street lights, wires and trees.

Abhiyansh clicked Hindu Gods at unusual angles. Sabah used unusual angles for buildings.

Sabah spoke of both his red cars from the past with ample animation. He was born in the undivided Hindustan, in Zila Rohtak, now in India. The fort there belonged to his grandfather, then the head of the Siddiqui family. For a small span of childhood, he lived in Dehradun. He once demanded a very expensive red toy car from his dad. At 76 when he recited this story, he sported a wondrous smile for this particular anecdote; "my dad did get me the car". Obviously, he had carried that joy along through his old age too. It was a lovely car, his pride, as he trailed it through the endearing mountains. An expensive wish coming true gave him a life skill-you aspire and dreams do come true.

He had arrived in the United Arab Emirates as a young man from Pakistan to explore work, leaving behind his young wife. All that he carried from back home were dreams in his eyes. And those eyes always remained gentle and loving. And honest! He chanced upon his first assignment from a Sheikh perched on a boat one fine day who asked if he could design a boat. He could, par excellence. His sketches and hand-drawn measured drawings were approved and fetched him good 500 Dhs. The first luxurious object he bought, after buying basic amenities for himself was a ring for his wife costing 200 dirhams.

In just a year or so, he was joined by his young wife. The diamond ring was loose and came off while splashing in the sea another day. Mrs Sabah cried inconsolably and Mr Sabah assured her of a new ring. Later the couple they were picnicking with pointed out at the shiny circle in the water. Mr Sabah said it was his "mehnat" in Urdu. It couldn't go waste. "Savaab ki kamayi" remained his belief throughout.

The children they bore were four beautiful spirited sons but Sabah sighed for a daughter. The youngest one responded well to music as a child and once pointed out a flaw in the flow of a live rendition. This one is going to be an artist, the dad declared, and so it happened.

Whenever a visitor to the office would ask about his annual earnings or would make a figurative assessment about his wealth, "billions" he would say with an assertion. His four able sons were the "Savaab" he said he had earned. He had earned so much that his lap was full and he was grateful to the Lord. With lovely curls and an accent acquired from an American university, speaking fine Urdu laced with an American accent, the youngest lad turned out to be a fine boy too and was to take over his business gradually.

He had bought a red car in Pakistan and spoke passionately of how he took it on a journey abroad to Turkey and finally to Europe, through the shortest route across the continent. Ria found this story of his, very fascinating, that of a world where you could take your red car into any country on a whim without the visa, without having had to stand in a queue in the embassy. She loved to envision his journey in the red car, while he spoke of visiting five European countries. The political boundaries and complications were inconsequential in his stories.

He always dreamt of the same world- a world he had experienced, without borders. Whenever he got nostalgic, he spoke about the havoc of Partition. He nurtured an almost personal grudge with Pt. Nehru over several reasons about how his nation got divided. Any political discussion, for further than three minutes there would emerge a name, that of unforgivable Pt. Jawaharlal Nehru. That would result in a closed-door argument or a discussion on Kashmir. He would slide the door between his cabin and the conference room where Ria sat. The Kashmir he spoke of, the peaceful one, of you in the valley, where if you uttered wow, it wouldn't be audible even to yourself. Would slip in the mist, mildly and hushed, just a sigh!

Ironically his birthday fell on November 14th, the same day as of Pt. Nehru's and he never mentioned about this connection.

Once a friend of his had asked for the car and hadn't returned it for a long time. When he had gone back to Pakistan to fetch his wife, the friend's mother failed in hiding the dishevelled spare parts and that was the end of his second red car and a story of rage not forgotten to date. Out of the window, went the friendship and trust. Ria wondered if that also added up to the reasons for his permanent move to the Emirates.

Well, his love for cars never weaned off. He was a proud owner of a Mercedes in his prime. Now he didn't drive anymore. In an accident a decade back, his having suffered a heart arrest, caused by the gushing of blood in anger and shock at the young boy who post hitting, picked an aggressive fight. Now not on the driving seat, he remained a lover of mean machines on wheels. Also, post recovery, he had started taking it easy. Since then, he had stopped being by the wheel and was driven around. "Tumhari Amma" he said to visiting Shehzan, his youngest son's enquiry about who had dropped him in the absence of a driver.

Another one of his stories was about his eldest son getting himself selected in a prestigious institute in the United States of America for education. The money had to be arranged. For several days, he woke up for Salat al-Fajr, without considering his health. He attributed the call from the Sheikh of Ras- al-Khaimah as an answer to those prayers. He was invited by the Sheikh's office to document his personal properties.

Sabah sent his son to study abroad and drowned himself further in the work with full gusto. He gained close access to the Sheikh's retinue and as a creative input went on to adding value and detailing of the house too, besides his own work. He asked Ria to fill the rest of the wall with the images of "virgin beaches of the emirates" as he called them. There were actually quite a number of beaches that were cleaned mechanically on a regular basis and didn't see many people visiting them while highly publicized and popularized beaches of Jumeirah were shallow and safe but populated with tourists. It was also blockaded after a certain expanse on each side of the vision, while the other beautiful ones were not.

In this foreign land, wherever one met people of Pakistani origin, they felt like cousins to you, only with a more polite language, more "adabb" as Ria felt. And Sabah's stories grew on her.

Didn't India and Pakistan seem more like cousins, long lost and angry at each other? Enough has been brooded about the losses in the past. Unimaginable losses caused by deceiving outsiders! Wasn't it time for the family reunion yet? Why not rewrite the future and close what was wronged in the past, mostly by external iniquitousness.

To feel the visual quality of the built form and capture it in an image also required a deeper understanding of architecture. The studio studied about it on a regular basis. Along with being the flag bearer about the importance of history, Sabah kept himself abreast with a deeper study of architecture to capture in the images the visual quality of built form in relation to the fog and sand.

Since Sabah liked to talk incessantly, Ria stopped entering his studio in the last hour of office. He had mastered the art of not taking a gap between his sentences, only put commas and the stories came out reeling, not preferring to end. Ria eventually plopped herself comfortably on the sofa in his office and soon his stories spoke of happiness in case she did not succeed to run away that day.

He daydreamt and insistently spoke about visiting the fort in Rohtak, his birthplace and the valleys of Dehradun where he spent his early childhood. He pined and rued about visiting India. Visa to India had been repeatedly denied to him. He visited Pakistan annually, attended to the repairs and sanitation, but had no intention of retiring there. UAE was his home for good and bad. Something had given his gait a weak limp the other day. He had just returned from the visa office. Even after living for 30 years in this country, like all expats, he had to go and renew his visa every three years.

Sabah adored his daughter-in-laws and his grandson. He would often talk of Zayan, his only grandson. On Zayan's birthday, none of the staff members was present to take pictures. Ria was invited and she offered to take pictures. He smiled and indicated graciously to dwell in the scene, mingle and not bother.

He introduced her family to all the relatives- his entire affable clan was here. All smiling and soft speaking people- Ria was inundated by familial warmth with them. Little children and adults, oldies- Sabah giggled with every single person. She was wearing an anarkali sent from India by her mother, with arms showing bare. All the females wore stylish salwar-kameez. She wasn't conscious of her attire but could sense a few mobiles clicking her way. Shehzan, captured the customary cake cutting pictures with gusto in his Leica.

The office had taken an assignment of covering the international event at the estate, an annual project for the Sheikh who had liked the proposal. On the day of signing of the contract he was accompanied with his wife. The project got shelved coz when given a budget of one million dirham, he went aghast, saying he would not have anything less than four million dirham and left. Ria was stunned. He never returned.

People who have so much to do, in that fervour, are usually pressed with time. Our Ms Ria being one of them, she hastily reached back to her car post after picking up some stuff from the local stores. A car was wrongly parked beside her car had a paper pasted on the front screen with a phone number hastily scribbled on it. The rear-view mirror had several symbolic religious hangings and the dashboard was unkempt. "I am sorry Madame", said the voice on the other end and quickly he came over. An old man with a quick gait, white beard, coloured kandura not very prim, lots of beads in hands, apologized again in an impeccable diction and moved his car. She went on to her errand and forgot all about it.

Weekends passed by and the familiarity that sets in eventually in a new abode with a routine took shape. The scale of grief or happiness could alter; it was a perception. The thick hard line between "happy problems" versus "real troubles" was forgotten. The couple's weekend was completely spoiled. Everything seemed grim. Radisson had called to refuse the club membership and Marbella club hadn't yet called in for the membership. The sad couple stayed at home.

The phone rang, disrupting an afternoon siesta and the person on the other end asked where was her car parked. He was the same person she had asked a few days back to move his car around the market, in front of the mosque. He added politely that police would be arriving soon in order to issue fattura for the entire shopper's queue of vehicles parked in front of the mosque. That led to non-availability of designated parking to the worshippers.

She thanked him, adding that she lived a little distance away from the mosque and wasn't a frequent user of that parking. She was curious, nonetheless, and walked by the mosque later. He was correct, the police car did come and left tickets on several cars parked there. He turned out to be the Imam of the mosque and he had complained to the police. He himself had to struggle sometimes for parking at the time of the azaan.

When the Marbella club offered membership the next month the evenings got some routine.

Next unprecedented event was a call on the landline from a man, unabashedly saying- "I need Razia". She couldn't fathom that and probed him further. "What are you saying? Who are you? What do you want Razia for?" In crude Hindi and a mix of Urdu, he explained that he wanted Razia for himself. She couldn't believe her ears- somebody was calling over at her place and telling her that he wanted the girl who came to work in her house. It seemed inconceivable a situation she could have imagined dealing with. But then it was to be dealt with. Who was this man? What could she do against him? Before thinking all this over she summoned Razia, who seemed harmlessly unaware. Pretty face, an attractive woman, her green eyes instantly got scared with Ria's grilling. She begged non-guilty while trying to make sense of what had just gone horribly wrong. She had shared the landline number with a friend and that must have reached the horrible caller. She hopelessly believed that the employer would see pain clearly in those green pupils. Today again her being beautiful was more of a trouble.

Till you are unaware of being beautiful, you enjoy that better. And once you get to know how powerful that is, boon or benefit could also be attributed to it. And in her case, it was brewing trouble yet again.

Perplexed, she held her thoughts and called Sumit. He, being overly cautious, immediately asked her to get rid of the maid. The human quotient was trying to make sense of it in the way of logic and in emergency. "Just show her out" is what his verdict had to be. She was an immigrant and must not be holding her papers. Hiring her was on the other side of the law.

The woman standing in front of her was away from home, in a foreign land, away from her kith and kin, her soil, only bearing the reality to earn money and her own face, her own body, her beauty was her biggest distress. Standing in front of her mistress, guilty of the mistake of giving her employer's number to a friend coz she didn't own a mobile. How could God, or who so ever responsible could be unfair to be sending her again to the big bad world? Razia's translucent green eyes looked the most painful pair ever seen.

She asked if she could call her friend from the phone. Ria couldn't let anything go wrong with herself, with Sumit's career. It seemed a simply goofed up situation brought up by that single, completely uncalled for, phone call. In distress Razia went to the cafe to call up her friend.

Sumit too was worried about the situation and any possible implication it could cause and disrupt the order just formed. He firmly repeated his decision.

The sore day had to see her out within a span of an hour from the time of the unwanted call. Back home this girl said, her husband would sometimes beat her up badly for money. If there was no money, he would barter the sack of grain or utensils for liquor. Amidst her repeated pleading and offering promises of not sharing the number again, Ria started packing groceries from the kitchen for her, which Razia would be needing immediately. She packed two big bags, gave her five hundred dirhams, and made Razia disappear from her house with a heavy heart.

Nevertheless, at this point she could only shed one tiny tear for her. The phone bell rang again and was from an emphatic but worried Sumit in between his work, but he also knew that they had reacted prudently in this foreign land.

Ria and the Imam ran into each other a few times while crossing the piazza in front of the mosque on the way to the art area —piazza with a single tree. She started learning Arabic from him. After a few times that she went to the side room in the mosque, he requested her to come wearing a dupatta.

Arabic is a soft language and requires sounds from the throat. Picking of words was easy but the sounds were a challenge. Few sounds had to initiate from deeper than the throat. The oesophagus, larynx, pharynx, trachea, respiratory system or whatever could Ria think of, it was crazy. And definitely, not an easy task to master!

Retro fitting of the entire art area through the museum, bookshop, restaurant, and art classes were adding verve to the historic complex. The adaptive reuse of the historic buildings while maintaining the ancient alleyways, built fabric and streetscapes, rather than just isolated buildings, gave a descent and synthesis into modern urban landscape.

Between the fine arts society, arts area, art institute and the like, the narrow and winding alleys became interesting walkways. These narrow passages she had clicked in Rajasthan as well. Ancient architecture and engineering had used this ingenious system to funnel the air, drop off the desert sand and cool the air.

The subtle nuances of light and colour in the sky were like those of watercolour paintings, with a unique luminosity.

When a thought takes you distances, unknown too sometimes ..

Walking alongside the other day was this man who seemed to be keen on a conversation in the club. A polite "I am not so keen in talking" look didn't help much. He spoke about his sojourn with the camera, next time she met him in the park. Otherwise, he was a banker.

The walk buddy got all the formalities done in a jiffy in a bank on the bank street. She opted for a smaller locker in the application form. Nothing like a speckles cellar that she was shown into and the small locker turned out to be of bigger width than the size of cabin baggage. It had a moulded briefcase inside consisting of several small boxes. It was horrendously bigger than her expectation and one of the tiny boxes held all the little pieces of gold and diamonds she had brought in this land.

She entered the office post the formalities, pretty late and talked about the size of the locker. George asked for a mithai and said this is kind of super natural news. "And why so?" Because we have never heard of anyone get one in this country, which has no locks in the cupboards. That reminded Ria of the rooms in the London apartment too, not having locks. Nevertheless, the office demanded mithai till she complied.

You play games with the camera sometimes. Read exposure, let ISO absorb a little bit of shock- like the shocker of a car. With a tripod, the image stabilisation feature needs to be off when shooting at low shutter speed. Don't go below 1/ 30th of a second since the hands do not remain stable. The masters raved about the light, since they practiced their art like a painting, the skill harnessed with the medium of light.

With her gear she came back to the bank and across the Naboodah house restored in the 1990s that belonged to the pearl merchant by the same name. The restoration was carried out well in time and the minimum damage was taken care of. The central courtyard and ramps led to rooms on all sides. The barjeels in this house weren't barjeels per se. These were wind scoops embedded in the walls. The floor seating at the end of the verandah, seen only in this one house now, had traditional floor seating exhibited, complete with decorations and accessories.

And on the flip side, exciting too was the upcoming rotating tower in Dubai, to be shot as an assistant to Sabah. The building was designed around light movement, like a sparkle in someone's eye. Light, like a dual personality, is the matter of form and energy both. And being a photographer's resource to control, manipulate, exploit at whim. Valuing the superlatives.

From the relentless power of full sun over water, the artists befriend, understand and read light. Light, through its character and quality, percept the photograph.

Sabah could appreciate straight shots too. To add brilliance as a photographer, the eye should rest at a point in a landscape picture. But her travel was restricted now.

On way to becoming a mother, she had another being to take care of. The camera, always an extension of her body, if not a part of it, was getting heavier week by week. Getting used to a life grow inside you was a little alien thought at first. Sometimes the realisation even scared her a bit; slowly it made her feel like a nurturer, a giver. It was kind of divine, too. Thankfully it was mostly latter than the former. She told this to Sumit who listened to it with a lot of attention and not with disbelief.

The camera – the extension and a companion, was also an object now. She had taken herself off away from me; the camera complained - and left me in the closet, sometimes without my cover and I felt uncared for. Few days I had spent without even seeing her. This life form went with Ria wherever she went and sometimes in his/her own sweet wish played soccer in the bearer's sleep.

Now Ria pondered over the power difference between genders. She could nurture, grow a baby in her. Sumit got her a book on pregnancy. "Enjoy the God feeling" written on it in his handwriting.

My child

Is a person – small indeed

I don't want to bend him –to touch my feet

I want him to grow towards light

And myself to reach a height

Where his heart holds me well

And depths, we should reach together, of bonding and understanding,

As fellow human beings!

It wasn't just a baby they made, a promise too. They would rear him as an excellent person; enforce values and strength for his flight. With peace and love ingrained which could always be carried along or returned to.

CHAPTER 10

Valuing

As if sometimes, for years you wait for the right person to understand some words, or to listen to theirs! For those exchanges of few sentences being plentiful. And making the time impeccable!

Abhiyansh:

It is so important to identify the state of emergency and normality. Aica who learned to live in a heightened state of work, constantly, lost the perspective of normal. Glorifying that busyness had become her normal. Talking to that little voice inside and talking to my own self was a bigger necessity when lost in time, when anything from gloom to business could be glorified. But it was gone.

With you, I was me

Now, I am different.

You took away a part of me.

I didn't have the luxury of making new memories, where ol' ones could keep fading, new being added. I collected all the moments like pearls and strung them together. A beautiful pearl line would have adorned her lovely neck if she wished.

I had gone weak in my knees concerning Aica. When somebody brings out that best side of yours, you start believing in the starry eyes adding a twinkle to your own prospect.

Everything exists in sets; there is never a single reason. With actions getting definitive, the world starts revolving around you. All is intertwined! Even luck is the pinnacle of the mountain, standing atop a heap of many factors. Luck just wasn't this plain and simple......so weren't you.

I have tainted all your places

Tainted them with passion

Your hill breathes my voice

The terrace by the lake whispers my music

The moon by the valley rakes in my graceful charm

The distant trees too look similar to those in the memory's background

Carry me along in the heart

So I let your places untainted

And in my heart, I carried you. I am not sure what and where will we revisit, hand on my heart in the dazzling lights, dissatisfied.

Forgetting seemed easier with ample immersive stuff around. I wanted to remember her. Wanted to keep her alive in me.

Finally, out of the clouds, I walk in the stormy skies, one muse to another. With only the sensation of the bosom mingled with the beauty of the night.

And I remember the last conversation with Ria before she had left. She offered her the hand. I took hers in both of mine. No words were actually exchanged before a quick side hug.

*****

When Aica left, he couldn't get angry. And when you can't, you feel lost. That was self-imploding, finding its way in the form of hurt. And poignant work for a few months before work and laughter got back on track. Forget he could not and moving on had to be endured. In the journey, the portions from memory worth treating and pondering about, retained gradually and the rest evaded.

Whatever he did wasn't good enough for Aica...but the goodness in continuation had to be maintained irrespective of the hurt or grief it endured.

"She was pretty, right and courageous. We men would have been happy to do anything for her. Somebody could go and tell her the power she could exert on us. To avoid ugly glitches and to do wonders."

"You want the selective best from a passionate person. How can that be! You will have to deal with the craziness too. Deal with it, sail deep and high both". She had said that to the 'me' that I was, then.

"Just be there to take me in or let me go spread myself.

Either you act or you sit on the other side to judge. The one you dream of, admire, remains admirable when you keep that distance. If you get closer, it takes effort too to keep the admiration working."

Was it or was it not about valuing and getting valued too?

CHAPTER 11

Suryansh

How quickly or how slowly one wants a chapter in time to tread, is in one's own hands. She paced it slowly, taking in the entire scene. Time that is immeasurable, time at her behest. Enjoying the safety of motherhood, splurging and cumulative, up to the brim. The more she revelled in the present tense, the more gladsome she was.

Now again!

An Actuality better than a musing

They were getting used to fitting into each other's lives. Suryansh, a tiny cuddle ball in her arms and she, an inexperienced mother. He would usually be awake in the early evenings and be sleeping most of the day. One particular evening, he was awake in the nursery, Ria watching his softness and glow, sun rays at a slant from the west-facing window. She got up to bring the camera but stopped taking in the experience of the serene delicacy. Indulging in the moment intuitively, she let go of the thought of a camera and rested herself beside the baby, in a caress you reserve for the most soft and fragile. And they both dozed off. It was so calming, silently fulfilling, never experienced before.

"My three fingers supporting, the little finger taking care of yours and also the ring finger. My thumb inclined on your hand as a trophy. What a frame! The horizontal line of the window panelling and that of the pillow trying to converge in imagination at a further end, the second soft pillow forming a curvature around my arm." The softness of the baby forming shadowed crests in the lit sheets and base of the arm resting profusely in the shadows. She lived this picture and closed her eyes. 'Will touch this picture sometimes, for now, it will dwell in my eyelids', thought she. Too precious to be stored anywhere else.

They bonded in a way that the hearts started communicating with each other and became two children together or maybe equals, for a few years. The car boot, besides holding the folding chairs and a bar-be-cue set, now had a baby cot, a perambulator, toys, kid bag and much more. The baby harnessed in the car seat in the back, diagonally opposite to the driving seat and his bags of endless requirements. The house too had more of his stuff than theirs, altogether put. Even the rearview mirror now had another tiny one under it, to check on him.

Young tot strapped onto the perambulator; Ria tried to resume her ambling by the beach. Every muscle of hers shrieked and she sat on the park bench on the way, before making it to the beach.

Human beings are social animals but in co-existence, they are a difficult species. A burqa-clad woman was already seated on the bench. In a few minutes, the tiny tot started giggling with the woman. Something had made her distraught. Ria brought her home, learned her story, and made a few calls to check. She mentioned about her previous employer who was so lonely, she would sit and draw in kids' colouring books and now had left the country for good.

Mumtaz was living with a few other Bangladeshi women. Sponsored by locals, as the prevalent arrangement would have it, females from the subcontinent were hired at obnoxiously low salaries. They went absconding after getting an exposure to the fair salaries. This had become the unsaid norm to make a living as illegal. How then, they were able to reach the Forex outlet was beyond Ria's understanding.

Mumtaz took to their home as fish to water. She would go back in the evenings to her shared accommodation or the hideout.

Living a day, an art in itself, how could it go by, just like that! There had to be something striking about the day. So, the conversation usually in the evening started with" What was best about today?" Out of all, the best was usually an anecdote- a set involving Suryansh, or his exploration, extremely satisfying at times. But could she let go of her vocation?

Sometimes, when Ria wasn't up to driving, the taxi drivers of Dubai that she experienced were a helpful and cheerful lot. Mostly from Pakistan with families residing back home, seeing a child gay and active, usually made them initiate pampering chitchat. The happy buddy landed up with a small toy and once even a car decoration hanging from the rearview mirror. These as gifts, the mother could not bring herself to say no to. Their Punjabi was sweeter than the Punjabi of people residing on her side of the border and the laughter was warm. Only when you were home in either of the nations, you were surrounded by that hatred for the neighbouring country.

Sumit started using the DSLR and the lenses. They had a new inspiration.

Mumtaz and Ria formed a rapport deeper than the throes of the usual housework. More than an employer-employee relationship, the alignment delved into a woman-to-woman connect. The day started with Ria moving her body from the bed and within minutes plopping onto the blue sofa, Mumtaz following her with a tray of ice cream, the Sudoku page opened in the supplement section of gulf news and a pen. Suryansh was more of a live toy, one who owned a million other toys. The pace of the house, he set. And the ladies would play with this live toy, Mumtaz too replicating his naughtiness and laughter.

Ria got herself books and read. She read to the child too. He was keenly interested in transport and very soon learned about the titanic and solar cars. The boy had a gala start of the day- sitting on the sill- looking out of the huge window- where he could see zooming cars, ships in the sea and aeroplanes to and fro. What a window for a little fellow! In a span of two years, the number of forks and knives grew to six to dig into the Cinnabon roll.

Suryansh got her interested further in cars and the thrill of speed. He could recognize Devil 16 prototype, Lamborghini hurricane, Donkervoort.

The car cleaner rang and started crying when she opened the door. A lady, he said, in a building en route to the art area had lost one child, threw another one in a blanket to a waiting crowd before she jumped too to escape the fire. He cried, reciting what he witnessed. To these people, away from home, a person's pain troubled more and then empathy was sought. The next day she read the same story in a newspaper. The cleaner came many a time after that but looking at him, she felt uneasy. She stopped opening the door and always tried to give his monthly salary outside.

Once at the beach on a Friday, the one towards Sahara mall, frequented by families, Sumit spread out the mats and chairs. The aroma from the bar-be-cue overpowered his senses. The whole area was lined with families out with bar-be-cue stands. Suryansh wandered off to the group nearby and returned with big shawarma in his hand to his parents' mat. Sumit's face gave an alarmingly disapproving look, seeing his son coming with the shawarma in his hand and it quickly turned into a look of disbelief as Ria took a bite. How could she let their child eat from strangers? Ria said because he had not spent so much time with the "strangers" in that country, like her. She took another bite ignoring Sumit's exasperated look and offered to send the courier guy again to get one for him. Well, the two of them ate in merriment, without looking at the angry member of the family. To be hearing about friendly experiences and culturally relating to them, were two different things for him. Nevertheless, he decided to collect recipes.

Soon, the young mother also started carrying extra goodies in her bag. Elders in public places, malls, museums, and parks alike would offer a packet to the random kids playing along with their own.

Between the wooden stacks of names like Pablo, Veronese, Hieronymus Bosch, inspiring silence broken only by prayers, she concentrated on writing, contemplating. Suryansh played with his truck books.

It was a juggle between keeping Suryansh occupied and wanting to know why Bosch left no letters or reminiscences. And later what were the explanations filled by speculations from his disturbed mind to his records of being a respected member of society?

Suryansh screeched and the mother ran to involve him with a cupcake from the cafeteria so that she could get more time to admire "the Garden of Earthly Delights." His spirit in terms of technique and imagery, he could have composed and given......

Suryansh ran along the corridor.

She wondered about the composition of the Creation. About God contemplating in the top left corner about his own creation of the world. The merger of real and imaginary animals! What thought went behind in the creation of unicorns as a myth of purity and so on.....

Suryansh started jumping.

The dark, chilly painting of the Death of Marat by Neoclassical painter David, the paintings taking them closer to photographic precision. The use of camera Obscura for proportions and accuracy, by artists like Durer, with accuracy. Also, Durer's fascination with producing self-portraits, an obsession she was inspired by in taking her own pictures.

As a gift, she asked for a day where she could sit in the library, take out books on paintings and study them. Suryansh too wanted his share of the gift.

"Garden of Eden" by Era Angelicia was superbly richly patterned. She couldn't completely agree that Eve's look was of dejection after having had the apple. Neither did she think the same for Adam's. Maybe society in general, like the painter, made it out? Somebody out there must have painted the celebration of the apple too, she imagined....

Suryansh became an imaginary land cruiser.

Diagonal light always reminded her of blessings and touch and as serendipity one saw in the powerful presence of God.

Red Canna reminded of deep poignant love....

Suryansh shrieked again.

Now the courteous lady at the desk, who had earlier given thick and big crayons to the kid, threw them both out.

The next Arabic class was at Imam's place adjoining the mosque. He introduced her to his entire family- a count of his numerous sons, not followed by Ria, in their rooms with a curtain on each door frame.

Negative space photography was required to be shot by her as an assignment before she resumed office. "Less is more" as is said. It was about the application of an imaginary grid in geometric form, in a minimalistic way. And venturing out picked up pace again.

Suryansh obsessed over cars and along with him, the mother. It was a game in the parking lots. Seated in his perambulator he would point out at a car, screaming the name and the mother would walk, go to the rear side of the car and verify the name. He was never wrong. And the drives of Sheikh Zayad, with "Onin" playing, as Suryansh called music, had all become sacrosanct. And the need was to push herself away, to work.

Aviation club had Zakir Hussain playing tabla. Sumit did not want to join. The aviation club OAT invited music enthusiasts. The sky went dark with pale thunder and people looked up. From the back entrance came in the light and out came bright traditionally attired musicians, playing the musical instruments, with each onlooker gaping. The hypnotic troop of musicians in a short procession to the stage and the stage lit up with an already seated team with the tabla maestro seated in the centre, his white shawl and kurta, curls and audience.

The metronome was perfect here, including that of the pace set by the thundering clouds. Zakir Hussain commented that Indra God was happy and blessed them with intermediate clouds thundering. The weather, space, lighting mood -it was a culmination of all the elements to perfection. Architecture, music, rhythm, space - all gelled well and produced a harmonious major confluence.

In a trial to resume outings without the child, Sumit was pulled along next time to Shaan's concert. The metronome and tempo were different this time. The concert started with a very new voice of the industry, Atif. For what was extensively melodious in his voice later heard, the same did not reverberate on that evening. Next came Shaan onto the stage and set the instruments, synchronized with the sound systems, keeping alive his dimpled smile. Always a fan of his song "Tanha Dil", Sumit wasn't aware of the dancing skills of his favourite singer. So much so, he joined the crowd on the side ramps in dance.

Ria got herself more books, oscillating between need to separate and connect. And she hadn't read in years.

Once you taste love, it becomes difficult to forget the feeling. It enriches you and binds itself in you. Plato spoke of the "ladder of love" by which the lover can ascend to direct cognitive contact with beauty itself, in his theory of symposium. In the Phaedrus, love is revealed to be the great "divine madness" through which the wings of the lover's soul might sprout, allowing the lover to take flight to all the highest aspirations and achievements possible for humankind, of higher pursuits.

Rumi, the great philosopher and scholar became a greater poet after he opened up to love through his encounter with Tabriz. Love and communion raising you to the highest level of meditation! The communion was through the souls or bodies or put together with the mind too.

Sumit was required to work extra time on Valentine's Day. Not wanting to fill in the evening, without him, she surfed through the show window of stylish small stuff.

She picked a lovely hand-crafted set of chess and two of the most exquisite cup, saucer and spoon sets. The spoons specially were fashioned in the way of a floral stigma, long style and petite ovary of the flower. Sitting on the saucer besides the cup with petals unwinding themselves in subtle curves and pastel appearance. The weather was pleasant the next morning. She set up a tiny table for two. For the smooth and the placid, she was the tempest.

And were there more sentiments and their susceptibilities that she was not akin to yet?

Suryansh was excited at the prospect of someone staying with them, family friends from India. They organised the house till it started looking perfect for a home stay. The toy room looked meticulously set up. Each animal parallel positioned against the next one on the wide blue sill with a neat Matt metallic finish. Suryansh would sit in the jungle to play "the birthday of lion", role-playing the monkey himself. Soft pine wooden racks from Ikea housed all kinds of vehicles neatly. The room always looked inviting; whenever a guest was over, he would hold the guest's hand and insist on them sitting in his squeal laced action room.

Suryansh would not stop kissing and hugging Tina. Ria and Tina planned itineraries. Among other plans, a visit to Burj-Al-Arab was booked on Friday.

Al Muntaha, the cantilevered feature of the mast inspired building, the finesse in its folded shape, viewed from the side and being clutched by the tower, was an imagery of finesse. Imagery of the long cantilever, replete with the base of a never still ocean below, constantly kept transmitting energy through waves and producing exciting sound of the surf and a tall offset of sky in between.

Gradually, with the kid growing up, there seemed a need for a social setup. She joined the 'get-together' group Poornima introduced her to. Jena, one of them, extended an invitation for dinner.

Her residence was a villa at Palm Deira, a man-made island built on reclaimed land. The fronds, the access, the infrastructure, the monorail, everything!

The ladies were all gathered around a large circular wrought iron table in the verandah on the backside. The side lane opened to the pool where people stood drinking collectively in a closed group. The round table, housing an equally intricate lamp in the centre, lit up just enough, with patterns to add drama to the conversation. Jena emerged in a satin black dress, looking plump and satisfied. It was a mixed group, some ladies Ria knew from an earlier introduction, expat neighbours of Jenas.

One drab topic of conversation after the other went on and it turned out that the husbands were an inescapable topic here. Jena concluded over her own husband's tendency of doing big and small stuff for her, pampering ones. Followed by oohs and opinions by others. Then the conversation moved to international topics, people from all over the world being neighbours here.

The garden ahead led to a long stretch of steps and further more to your own private stretch of the creek. It was a gorgeous night. There were few lights shining dimly in the villas and fewer on the opposite side of the creek with an exorbitantly bright moon above. This was unlike the light polluted usual UAE. The darkness around and the awesome setting of the dim lighting with only your imagination perhaps, matched the flux apt for the party. You could see each other, admire the details and Meetu did not let a prick comment on Ria's dress.

The more she tried to have real conversations with many in this group; it kind of failed and made her feel inefficient. Also, something was wrong with these parties when eventually men and women sat separately. She got up to see what Sumit was up to. Suryansh was that same little clingy fellow which situations like these made him to be.

She guessed it was inherent for the child to feel the way parents feel, somehow. Sumit was ill at ease with his company. She took the child from him and tried to send him with the other kids who were going to the dark sandy beach. The overtly careful child did not want to leave her. Poornima and a few other females started towards the beach too. She tried to gauge Sumit, who wanted to go back.

If only they could sit on the beach and take pleasure in one of the most exotic locations in the region. It seemed too perfect a setting to not soak into. The party had anyway just begun; she could have gaily spent the entire night. The group of people by the beach would also have been a fascinating visual. But then, that was it.

Again, came Ramzaan, the special month. The evenings profusely action filled, the markets abuzz till late. This year long festive days had come in good weather. Sumit would reach home everyday by afternoon, draw all the drapes in the entire house and spread sleepy germs everywhere. The wife and the kid would fall in his trap, after he cuddled, coaxed, lulled, pampered, and acted sleepy with such conviction. Post the doze, it was a rush-rush getting ready and zooming out, as the iftaar time would be nearing. People would gather inside the mosque, systematically and patiently sitting in queues. Pavements also would be lined up. Mats were spread and plates and food and drinks, mostly laban and dates, were laid in front of everyone. It would be Azaan and Ria could share a sigh of relief for the hungry. Traditionally Roza was opened with a date.

On the roads one could see sheer madness of speed before that, drivers trying to make it to the iftaar scenario and settle down before the Azaan.

Now, this was also a time to rush outside, while most people were busy in the iftaar. You could get on the road and drive like a racer. Twenty minutes to reach the City Centre in Dubai, which was one fifth of the usual time. A new comparison sheet started to build up between Iftaar driving time vs non-iftaar timing.

The local bazaars, the souq and the malls - it was festive everywhere. The road sidelights were patterned in celebratory shapes over long days of festivities.

The display of colourful merchandise in the local souq was enormous. Without the partitions and glass facades of the modern souqs, this one was a little distance from the buildings, frequented by displayed Arabic calligraphy. The small square stained glasses in the roof were imported decades back from Istanbul and the logs of sandalwood in the roof above the central seating were from India. The pearls and corals took to the visitor's fancy.

The buildings here rose from the ground instead of sitting on them. While mostly ones around the art area seemed placed on the ground and farther ahead, they were out right ugly. The former ones had a poetic hierarchy. They invited you to explore the spaces enclosed, the spaces with open arms —containing its lyricism - a pattern could be felt through the language the designer had tried to speak in. The latter ones only cried for attention.

With Suryansh, new subjects were constantly in experimentation. The latest were of madly spun tyres and burnt rubber.

The New Year cracker show in waters of the creek was a conglomeration of human spirits in unison with an event just like the one besides the London Eye had been.

The dhows and Abras were all stationed that night. There was a sea of people as far as one could see. The fireworks on the deck in the creek greeted the newly arrived year amidst cheer, applause and a sense of bonhomie with the world in general.

The dance with males swaying in unison was a traditional one, a re-enactment of battles won. And quite a number of them dance with the smooth swaying sail of a ship as a metaphor.

Sabah's macro photography related to religious symbols, calligraphy, dhow against waves, and elements of nature. Next the protégée had to be trained to remove her shades and open the macro capability of the eye.

Delhi friends' worry about their tiny daughter's school admission rubbed on this set of parents too. Suryansh schooling wasn't bothered about yet. Followed by research, the school of the crown prince seemed appropriate. Just a visit and that was it. While Ria was busy with the accounts, the little one was engaged with the porcupine in a cage by the entrance. The porcupine was a big player in the decision making about the school. It was a little strange; the whole school affair didn't take more than a week and no effort what so ever. Discussing it with friends made it little stranger. They were celebrating that a school of choice had their little girl's name in the list back in NCR.

Ria's compositions nowadays were about stories around her child. She noticed the compassion he was encompassed with by people unknown. Random people friendly with children and they in turn playing with strangers, as if by intuition. The shoot of little people, mostly carried on inconspicuously, was summarised in short bedtime stories by the day end. The other night's storytelling ritual revolved around the motion blur created with stabilizing of hand with 1/10th of a second

Adults and little people's interactions started showing up in the frames now. The life values Ria and Sumit wanted to teach the son were forming in their discussions.

Modelling a puzzle maze for him on the bed for him to take his cars around, it looked confusing about who was being raised by whom. She declared to all her friends in India that life was perfect, didn't want a shade more or less. Sumit was trying to keep up with the energy in the house. And of course, joy rubbed off on him too. Ria took it upon herself to fill in the father with details of growing of the child, so he wasn't left out and gelled well with the energetic duo.

The rose-coloured glasses were coming off. To be replaced with clear scratch less ones. All of this was no longer a want, it was a need, and much like the air she breathed. What was that in the distance, unable to be read with these glasses?

CHAPTER 12

Longing

Whatever was said and unheard, was formulated in full force now. It excited, confused and flummoxed Ria, especially because she was used to being in the moment rather than in the past.

It made her gasp, breathless. And inextricably so! An unexplainable colour dawned, a complex one. Only if longing could find a tangible colour to adorn, to attribute itself to, as it was now slightly surfacing in luminance. And quickly drowned too, irrevocably. With all its sensibilities or morose lack of them. But it did hit! Abundantly.

Did he deserve to be intensely remembered, now? Delving into it! Now? Requited or unrequited was out of the question. Those were suitable times in retrospect. Fun, reckless, exciting, full of hope! And wasn't being lovelorn better than not having experienced it at all. She was a muse. What if she had a muse! With a sudden force, she understood his perplexed incertitude of overlaying a muse with the one gone by. But even with her not understanding it, wasn't he as an artist supposed to take care instead of letting go completely. What she had momentarily experienced and didn't pay heed to was making sense, now that she had matured herself as an artist.

I woke up in my sleep to converse with you in my thoughts.

How about a conversation over coffee in the day!

Him:

I didn't have the luxury of adding new memories and fading away from the old ones. The pearls collected were strung now.

A dainty pearl line would adorn the time memory or the lovely neck, had Aica wished. Had Ria wished!

So was the desire the root cause of all troubles? It must also be the root cause of personal happiness, a basis of achievement. Why kill then-why not fulfil? What if I had let myself go ahead with this person who, besides touching me, enhanced my creative pursuits as well. And I could have become, a still more valued friend.

Her:

When I experience the excitement in a fancy place, I sometimes am reminded of the assignments with him in gravel, dirt, the constraints and the coarseness of sites. Joy could be equated between people, even in contrasting situations.

Did I have a craving then or was it now that I wished he had touched me!

Him:

I wished I had touched her once when I saw her face was sad. Now that face was distant in some another world, it was inconvenient to fathom "distant", so I settled for sad. That memory followed with the reminiscence of how her radiant smile charged the whole air around.

I can never look at the crimson zing red wall and not think of her. If I had captured her soft-looking shoulders, beautifully shaped. Prose started flowing naturally out of me and pushed the insides of my brain till I freed myself of them in a peppermint pink colour against a white backdrop.

It was difficult to deal with her. One couldn't build a strategy around it every morning. In the end, the butterfly approach had worked. Let her flutter and settle, enjoy her flight from the window as much as the time permitted and let her be. Just remain together and work it out.

It was a longing, more than 'reaching out and attaining'. And carrying that longing along, forever.

I wanted adoration again, she came along. And left with a longing, a long longing.

Aica:

"Couldn't' you be a taker, give back lovingly, feel loved and it could work out.

Why to find a keeper. Why not just in the moment, not waste your emotion on them……………" Abhiyansh couldn't read Aica's last email further. He had never been able to.

"If I can feel oneness with you, it's not me who is blessed, it's you who is blessed……for I love you so," he had scribbled on the side margins of her image and sent it. And I am thankful for this happiness and bonding and the pain and separation. One would give this experience away for nothing."

 Her:

"You could not bond with me freely; scared that I would then start expecting so?

Even if I did, what a beautiful expectation it would be, feeling loved by you in return. We can be compatriots in the journey, being a source of solace or happiness." Scribbled was this note in my diary.

When had I written it and forgotten? Was it an observation for some of the article I must be writing or a note for myself?

*****

It was beautiful…till it lasted.

Like the rain, the elixir.

You run out oozing with joy, the lips open and you feel buoyant. A drop falls into the mouth. A blessing.

Any form of expression where one was true to it, was magnetic, powerful, forcefully propelling till there was an outcome. So was a content relationship with a muse without disturbing the core.

But the loneliness of the heart traded for being lovelorn was always better.

Does the stimulus get a new face? Between staccato and legato. The music, as said, is made in the gaps and not by the notes themselves.

*****

Her:

Are you pining for me? You know that feeling. There are parts of you that you too want to explore. There are always unknown unknowns, boundaries, habits and deeply etched thoughts. Some in satiated creativity and some in wondering about them.

Him:

You are more important to me than work.

Lack of fodder doesn't stop my time; I look inward and thrive but the blooming rain of leaves and flowers seized. For longer than expected.

Her:

Yes, he could be irresistible-if one thought that way. But what awareness was pushing her into thinking so now?

Sometimes on the beach, the waves did make me think of him. Did I have a craving then or is it now that I wish he had physically touched me once.

Him:

This cotton candy blob, white and blue at edges, wanting to be caught.

Grey, not out of black plus white, grey as a mix of fuchsia pink and cobalt blue.

After running all over and enjoying being a nomad, this "ordinary" is what is alluringly extraordinary.

The serene white in the sky is slow, at peace with itself. In the magnitude of the earth's speed, it would be fast-moving, but to itself, it is beautiful and sure of itself.

I dreamt you would call up.

There is nothing to forget, Ria. When you breathe the other person, you fight with yourself. I breathe the ones I love. So I was arguing with myself.

My jealousy knows its bounds. There was a link between the orgasmic and creative juices, in appropriate settings. Some people work out this connect, few artists and muses too.

Her:

The pearl string has hung for too long

Waiting to be adorned by your hands

It smoothens on the neck in anticipation

On my own

I take one pearl and wear in my own hand in consolation.

Why suddenly you altered the affectionate stance, I do not know.

In a relationship, when one person decides to alter it and doesn't let the other one know- the other one surely suffers or gains.

Him:

I was not able to remove the guilt from my mind.

Wanted to reach out, but not to be asked for promises.

The earlier experience had determined that. The beautiful shady roads in the long drive had all become silent after he met Aica. And later the spontaneous charm of the meadows, the stone architecture, the purple leaves beaming out of the green ones in the ground cover, the one and a half feet red stone steps besides the brick structure without the railing, her beautiful face against the sill. With spontaneity gone, the cloud nine like setting also couldn't gladden the heart.

Psycho that she was, Aica always searched for symmetry and balance. She combined opera and ballet as her physical forms of expression. Her flair extended to being a ballerina and a photographer and a lyricist, besides being crazy. Travel was in her head, more than her feet.

When not actually travelling, she was ruminating through the history of places, travelogues, and war chronicles. Endowed with a petite figure she could get absorbed in a free-flowing dance or a pose of ballet anywhere. She complimented the stage or an airport lobby with equal sensation.

Aica couldn't sit down as a habit and would angle her limbs or her body, practising her moves. In their travels together she had provided enough shots, worth millions, of her engaging attention in the piazzas, front of monuments and immaculately grand interiors. Capturing her against these was an extension of the art itself. So the album had her petite silhouette around the whole of Europe, South America and Australia.

Tutus and leotards and pointe shoes against the exquisite backdrops made your hands fondle with the prints delicately.

Nothing gave her more boost than getting herself captured in a swirl in spaces with stringent geometries. Starkly dressed, hair tied in a bun, standing on points in arabesque and ready for her performance of Giselle, he also had a collection in his personal folder. She didn't even need to model. Bun coming off and the glamour of her hair let loose, frantically flying out with the wind, eyes inebriated by the same wind and a pose each time struck on its accord. He had to keep up constantly.

Commitment in personal relationships jittered her. And she did not understand this characteristic of hers. That suited most of her relations pretty well. Few days or months or years or even seconds. And Abhiyansh was confusing. For an artist, love could be in a moment but then there was the next moment. She said he was non-committal.

Him:

Why do I look outside?

For when I look only at us, you feel cluttered.

Some tiny voice inside said- it couldn't be so- future couldn't be like that- and slowly I bounced back.

Her:

Yes, he could be irresistible if I thought about it then, years earlier. Why was I remembering him now?

The eyes that pierce

The mind that dreams

The soul that flies

Him:

I have a need to be needed.

It was not like the river drenched in its own sound, squashing everything else. The flow strong enough in itself, taking the rocks too, further along or shaping them and moving on.

All I did was in complete consciousness. Even the tussle with Aica was in complete consciousness, not profane.

It was like the stillness of a meandering river, like the Brahmaputra, viewed from the top. Flanking tributaries from that distance and water flowing at whichever rate looked at peace.

If you could blissfully enjoy her music, you could even dance to yourself.

Her turbulence was the algae growing sloppily under me, the aqua green. I liked only those soft white ripples, moist tiny droplets flying out of them into the air.

You had to let her go. More the obstructions, more the ripples. He had enjoyed the white surf over the green coloured water. When one crosses over a river, the flow again becomes smooth and graceful. It was meant to be.

So many people lose after a lottery. Human nature knows how to deal with sadness. It is happiness that is difficult to behold, sometimes.

The fresh greens against the light looked brighter - emerging greens, very lightly hinted. Slowly they would colour and set in. March again, she should do the same – shed old leaves, renew with the new greens.

Relationships can make you feel rich or stupid and empty.

The strumming of this music would blow into a full symphony, maybe later.

CHAPTER 13

Mumtaz

Come summer and they went on a holiday to Europe. She pointed out the ornamentation detail to Sumit, a deja vu, of an image on Abhiyansh's table.

The splendour in its detailed version wowed them. A profusion of flowers against a background of cobbled stones! The beauty of drab colours in a pattern! Creepers in bountiful! A tangerine painted frame around a wooden door with a horseshoe handle! The lens kept changing. Macro photography had interested Sumit and now he wanted to shoot too. Two more cameras were bought. And the holiday turned into a friendly challenge of the shoot.

Stone, the soothing beiges skin brown, roughly textured masonry adding more flair to the texture, a narrow balcony above the door with space only for foliage.

The renditions of spaces on a scale, relatable to the narrow alleys, called for walks throughout the days. The tourist places were skipped. Watching out into the scenery and further on into nothingness, she became conscious of the influence of Abhiyansh's photography in her work. And the recognition of his thought process, while he must have ventured in those areas! It had seeped into her vision too.

A report of his, she must have saved somewhere with her stuff in Delhi.

Documentation of a week spent in a world of old-time charm, providing vivid visualisation of the pace of the city. And the research material about what would have been prevalent in the days of glory, a whole century ago. Architecture that sustains itself, as a reflection of the past and a perceptibility of the society at that time!

An elaboration of factors that led to the integration of the urban economy and social fabric with tourism was compiled. Also elaborated was the importance of the support of citizens as an act of comradeship of the community as a whole.

Ria did her brief write-up besides the visuals. The cafes with hard finishes and see-through cooking operations with the mayhem of cutlery made almost no sense in cities already in a cacophony of sounds. The organic farm café looking out into the greens and natural synthesis with country music or jazz playing in the distance and food served at a slow pace even, the localised sounds only added to the flavour of the place rather than the cutlery giving you a shriek at a slight drop.

Even in the finest of hospitality experiences, the music not relating to the sensory experience can leave it undersigned. And it can create confusion about a building being a hotel or a hospital. A hospital was required to exude hope and a hotel that of recreation.

On the way back, Sumit felt he mistook reading Dubai as Delhi in the boarding pass. Ria was already remembering India. A sojourn in a place of bountiful beauty and on the way back how you think of home.

Outside the Dubai airport, what started showing up now was uncoordinated dwelling and lack of aesthetics.

Abhiyansh, somewhere in the background, was now clearing up just like the blue sky!

Not the saturations, the streaks, the violence, none of the randomness.

Blue, the absolutely usual one, clear blue and puffy whites here and there.

The strategy did matter. For epic wars and for the routine! Backed up with reasons! It could take the form of tyranny in monarchs to oppression in the household.

Listening to Mumtaz's story made her wonder how people make oppression their way of living too. Many a time this oppression could be from a close one.

Between her books and photography, Ria started conversing with Mumtaz while the kid dozed. Why not break away and not spend her entire life with an ugly reality? If the oppressor wasn't one of your own, it was definitely easier.

Nonetheless, Mumtaz was a real life hero.

What is your problem "with it" demanded the old lady furiously in Arabic. The very imperative tone and pithiness put Mumtaz off balance. The younger son had beckoned her while she was ironing clothes. She simply followed him. When he had tried to grab her by the arm, she had been swift in running away after pushing away the man. Summoned by 'the mother', while her head still reeled and processed, she couldn't put up with the mother's brevity. The mistress's fury completely put her off guard. Any plea of right over wrong, ethics or religion was sure to fall on deaf ears, so she politely but firmly stayed put.

The infuriated mother warned her blankly, they would take her to the desert, kill her coldly and leave the body to rot. Nobody in the entire world would ever come to know about her remains. She would make sure of that so Mumtaz better agree after the son's hand had healed from the bleeding in the accident.

Mumtaz stole a little folding knife from the kitchen and from that day onwards started carrying it in her kurta. In the following days, she spent some of her fish frying time stitching pockets inside all of her kurtas. That pocket would always house her knife and later, her mobile.

Frying fish in the kitchen was anyway her favourite job before the incident. It used to give her some respite. It was also the least favoured job amongst all her comrades. The air conditioners were off-limits in the fryer kitchen, located in the extreme corner of the house, opening into the backyard. The whole of the villa was otherwise centrally air-conditioned, including the servant quarters.

The smell of fried fish had slowly become pleasant to her senses. The slime of the fish and the freedom from the prying, hostile eyes gave her a sense of herself. Also, the fish reminded her of home. Home in Bangladesh, tattered, green fields around, two sons squealing and fighting, roof in shambles.

She held herself together by husband's efforts, her mother-in law's hut in the distance, serenaded in memories. Memories and sighs!

With the door opening towards the rear open area to ward off the smell, it was a bliss of solitude. Ameena, her friend on the neighbouring terrace at a considerable distance, sometimes waved while spreading out the washing. She would wave back and chat.

Mumtaz saw her howling after a few days. She was alternating between howling and sedation. Allah wouldn't have forgiven. She took out the tiny notebook and scribbled. It took her a long time to write that one long sentence. "I have arranged for a driver to help me out of here on Friday Namaaz time." Ameena would have been the easiest bet to smuggle out but not the best, given her meekness. In the middle of the night, she hid the paper in the basket. Yusuf, the driver, used to bring fish from the backyard. He got the fish and carried the basket back to see the delivery to the next villa on

Mumtaz's request. That day's fish fries turned out to be crispier than usual.

Come Friday they were ready and counted breaths, each in her garden. Yusuf didn't arrive.

Was it worth creating another ruckus in her life? What of Abdul's future! To see him bloom into an able man, she had sustained so much. Baba the Arbab had already promised employment and a visa to her son. But did she really have to suffer at the hands of this family? She would not be able to hold back her grief if she saw him face to face next month on her deportation. But if she did not help Ameena and herself, would her mild manner let her sleep in her hut, in Bangladesh? She hadn't faced this kind of combat situation ever. Mumtaz faltered. She was responsible for herself now more than her concerned set of people and she did gain strength and risked her life. Cleverly, she added.

Well, cleverness was a very subjective thing.

This female proclaiming herself to be clever and speaking of such big an escapade as if it was a simple, off-handed banter was perplexing. Ria's horror and sting in the heart knew no bounds. And Mumtaz's self-belief and proclamation of being clever only added rapidity to the tears forming in Ria's eyes. This lady from the farms of Bangladesh standing in her living room, holding precious crystals, cleaning them for Ria, was a real-life hero.

Her flight from Dhaka in Bangladesh to Sharjah, a year back, was in the middle of the night. After being seen off by the agent, she enquired the fellow passenger, how long would it take to reach Sharjah. The fellow passenger pointed to the air hostess offering water and trying to help her with the seat belt. On getting to know that she was flying, Mumtaz created a ruckus. She wasn't informed of the mode of transport. The air hostess then assured her about being in an upscale bus, the only one that was high on speed. When she returned from the washroom, everyone was eying her amusedly and the co-passenger kept the window closed. When she stepped out, the air hostess told her that she was now in Sharjah and indeed had flown to the emirate, for coming by bus would have taken ages.

This naivety was Mumtaz's own measure and by now she took pride in having come a long way in cleverness.

She wondered if half the people in the world are good because of their children. And equally gone bonkers, like 'the mother' as the entire household called her, because of the children.

Abhiyansh's series of children's faces as sunny as sunflowers, as withered as labour. That he said was a reflection of a 'world- to –be' and a reference to the amends or preparations of the future. How relatable was that now? Ria shuddered and how even earth-shattering stuff is forgotten; the incident too was, in a few days. Only Ria became cautious with exposing Mumtaz to the front door.

There was a talk of the upcoming Masdar city near Abu Dhabi, which was to become the physical manifestation of sustainable development and spoken of highly for its zero-carbon target and the low environmental footprint. Sheikh Zayad too spoke of green buildings to become the norm in Dubai.

The family undertook a long drive to Al Ain in the emirate of Abu Dhabi to witness airplanes on show, post the talk. From the stand, the glider landed on a moving jeep, narrating which went on a repeat mode with Suryansh.

The skies and sand formed a backdrop to the formations. On the other side were a fleet of trucks, four-wheel drives standing majestic on the sand. People viewing the air show from the other side, in the desert sand, without having the crowd around, also made for good pictures.

Suryansh made a failed attempt at asking for a cold drink and was directed towards layered shakes and shawarma instead.

The rulers of the emirates of Abu Dhabi, Ajman, Dubai, Fujairah, Sharjah and Umm-al- Quawain and later on Ras-al-Khaimah, had united to form a single entity in the early seventies. Instead of celebrating independence from British rule in the late sixties, the UAE celebrates a Union day on the 2nd of December. It's a public holiday and is celebrated with much gusto. Carnival parade, folk bands, national operetta, skydiving shows, heritage cars lined up along the piazza at Qanat in the festive air. Stilt walker clown performances, acrobatics set the children laughing in the carnival parade before and after the national day.

Various events promoting Sharjah's culture and heritage were organized all around. Khalid lagoon, a week later, would see the finale of F1 powerboat world championship. The nationals, holding their hands, sang the country's national anthem. Waterfront lit up with spectacular fireworks.

Over tired but excited Suryansh had to be pulled back home. She could only catch a glimpse of unique colourful paintings. 38 young artists had collaborated in doing up 38 paintings to display the connection with the 38th National day. The country's obsession with "world's largest/biggest" had led to the stitching of the world's largest flag, to be displayed from the next day. The military band's rendition of national tunes instilled the same pride that the national anthem back home did.

This time Grishma on the landline disrupted her afternoon siesta. She on the other end began the conversation, asking about the whereabouts of her mobile phone. The sleepy head remarked it would be somewhere in the house. After a wait of one and a half day a guy in the kachcha parking had called a random number, which was Grishma's. The owner of the phone now got up sloppily and called her mobile number. The person at the other end exclaimed about the past one and a half day worrying him about the owner's worry. They decided to meet in front of Lulu, the hypermarket. Her red coloured child's stroller was a pointer for recognition. The sleepy head checked on Suryansh playing the tumbling train toy with his and went back to bed without a care in the world.

The evening stroll was to the supermarket for a cake and other regular goodies and then to Lulu. A person in his sixties wearing dull grey kurta salwar, holding a plastic bag, walked towards her. He was a taxi driver and had spotted the phone on the ground in the kachcha parking. The plastic bag contained 15-20 cold drink cans. He said he got those for the child, since she had mentioned the stroller. Suryansh held the cold tins in his lap with pleasure. She was promptly touched and thanked him with the small cake, which was luckily hanging in the plastic bag on the stroller. They spoke about his children back at home in Pakistan for a little while and he blessed the kid in the stroller clutching onto his wish come true.

Strange are the ways of wishes and prayers, this time his Bhagwan and Allah had conceded over a tiny person, Ria couldn't help ruminating on the way back to the house. She was overwhelmed and wanted a person to share this with. Suryansh was deftly given cold drinks to enjoy this time.

It rains in Sharjah:

It rains! Raindrops and astonishment outpour on people's faces. Descending drops split on the pane, making Ria and Suryansh run out onto the terrace. Together they pull Sumit and push him out of the house for a ride. When the car hits the water, Suryansh and Ria feel exhilarated with it splashing about and Sumit feels troubled, wondering if their humble car will make it through the flooding of water on the road. The country not used to rain had no water disposal plan either on the roads. Sans a smile throughout the drives he was.

The city was so unprepared for rain; the subways were full of water. Suryansh was a little confused but having a gala time nonetheless. Driving past the town, closer to the Corniche the flooding disappeared. Sumit was now heaving a sigh of relief, his predicament of pushing the car in waters being lifted off on the clear Corniche. Now he wanted his child to experience the paper boats and looked for puddles, settled on a large one between the road and the pavement kerb. His ability to be childlike with the toddler, never failed to melt Ria's heart.

The glee in the child's mannerisms was a scene to behold. O the family scene looked beautiful to the passer by with those white and black of the pavement, the puddle, two paper boats, a man still in his office attire and a child with curly mane, shrieking in excitement, and if you looked from a distance, a lady who had churned out this scene and was now capturing a faint dark glimpse of it, just for records, in a Nokia 1100 mobile phone.

Moments of baarish and flimsy boat sailing spent with the son. And there was something about the paper boats, which lost the shape and tore off in the water itself. The act of playing in the rain with the paper boat felt complete, with traces of paper gone and in evaporation of water too in a matter of time. 'Play, put it behind you and only take the enjoyment home.'

At the jewellery market, she did the environmental portraits and took them to the office. As is with portraits, the first ones seemed to be the best shot- the most random, appealing and speaking on their own. Often, the first or the last portraits of the same subject came out to be the best. The rest became a process.

The emirates were just not sleeping altogether in the Ramzaan month. Local young emiraties were out on the roads, visiting one another, hanging out by the restaurants and juice shops till the wee hours and woke up late in the afternoon. People like Sabah did not approve of that. They accepted the patience building side of the festival very seriously. He maintained his usual routine. The fasting was to imbibe tolerance with the self and then was to be rewarded with bonhomie and luxury.

Only practicing the enjoyment part of it was unacceptable for him. Ria opined that at least this got the youngsters in practice.

The feasts were elaborate as he described and invited Ria with her family to his house on Eid. He also described the zaqat - nobody would refuse a needy. While being seated on the huge warm Persian rugs the host the other day had taken a pile of notes from under the rug and passed onto the person sitting next to him after just a sentence was said. A decent fellow, who may have been his relative, kept the transaction as inconspicuous as the host. The genuine need was fulfilled, simply. He explained the meaning of Zakat. Some percentage of your earnings was supposed to go to the less privileged, unsaid, untold.

On Eid, at the neighbour's, the mother taught the lil' child to hug and wish. And to address Suryansh as "bhai jaan."

Post lunch Mumtaz said she had to go to the neighbour's house and was taking Suryansh along in her arms. Ria felt completely at loss of words. What could she say and what struck as horror in her mind till Mumtaz returned, she hardly breathed. Never again will the child be sent again alone with Mumtaz became clear to her, come what may.

Mumtaz could not turn up that day. Next morning she brought a friend along. The usual candour on her face missing, she offered some miffed explanation about the friend. The other girl too did not seem composed too. Still sleepy, Ria didn't give them much thought and went inside to nap.

Waking up to the sudoku routine, she went to have her coffee in the balcony. Mumtaz got a small bag of cloth and also took off her gold jhumkas, asking Ria to keep them for her. Now the unhappy look in her eyes was clearer.

Last night, at their place had come two young local Arab men looking for girls. The girls hid wherever possible. Mumtaz and another girl had not gone home but had stayed at another friend's place.

Apparently one of the girls called the police. She must be either new or very terrified. Calling of the police would mean taking all of these to the police station, verifying their status, throwing them in jail and deporting them. The poverty-stricken real-life heroes, who had left their children and life back home and been through the torture of the natives took that one-month of stay in the jail quite normally. The deportation was what they feared a lot. In most cases, they had taken a huge loan to pay to the agent and to buy the air ticket while coming. The low pay at the sponsor's house took more than a year to pay off that loan, provided the sponsor actually paid the money.

She asked Mumtaz if this was only with Bangladeshi women. She revealed that many girls from Kerala also followed suit. Parents and husbands sent them too in search of work through agents. So many of them got mishandled with the dream of a better life shattered. Few of them physically gave themselves in as in few cases the family back home got to know. If the girl returned home, it would usually be with a shattered dream.

The next day Mumtaz didn't turn up and through Nathur it became known to Ria that the phone call to police was from Mumtaz because of an enmity. The Arab men had come by chance and it had made everything more complicated.

Ria shuddered and went in shock. How close could one get to crossing the thin line between faith and trust and outrageous danger? She hugged Suryansh tightly and for a month could not feel secure.

How time lets things be unrestrained and then back to usual.

Tissue boxes and plastics in general were abused in this country. Out came the tissue box at the juice guy. India had started the shift against plastic bags long before. The milk, yoghurt, deserts, extra layer over soaps took so much of her bin space and she felt horrified at the number of plastic bags one brought from a single trip to Carrefour and Spinneys.

Slowly the mother and son, both professional window shoppers, became compulsive shoppers. They would both wake up to the plan of choosing one mall for the day. Even a drive on Sheikh Zayed road to spot the stretch Hummer in the fourth or fifth lane was a thrilling idea some of the days. He with his eye connects and continuous chatting made immediate friends everywhere.

Ayesha Saif Al Shamsi had her birthday in a week. This was the first invitation card Suryansh brought home from school. Lady's name was on RSVP. Ria called up and tried to strike a conversation with the kid's mother.

Apparently, she was one of the staff and Ria stated a confirmation.

Suryansh was pretty excited. His friend Mustafa was coming too. Friday evening both went over, leaving Sumit with his "me time." The address turned out to be a whole complex comprising of four villas set widely apart in a common boundary with lavish grounds, on the outskirts. The entrance had a five storeyed bouncy and multitudes of jovial kids.

Suryansh clutched to her and after some prodding by Mustafa, climbed onto the bouncy. She looked around for other moms. The other people accompanying the children turned out to be maids. The first garden had a big bouncy. Mustafa was on them. Ria greeted his mom who informed her that she was leaving the child and pushing off. All the other kids were either by themselves or with their attendants. She asked Suryansh if he would be fine to be picked up later. He blankly refused and pulled her along towards the allure.

On the other side of the road separating this garden with the rest of the green was an oval train track, half a thousand feet in running length with children of all ages, elders and the birthday girl riding on it. Further ahead there was also a crowd. A lovely lady, Ayesha's mother, greeted Ria. After sharing pleasantries, Ria remarked that it was quite a big party. She said it was a combined birthday party of Ayesha and her cousins. Cousins. As Ria later comprehended, were half- siblings as there were four mothers, hence the four villas in the complex.

The internal roads were a network and all the types of trucks one had seen on the roads were either parked or moving in the complex. Suryansh refused to sit on the huge train; Mustafa was happy trying out everything and talking in Arabic.

Suryansh decided clinging onto his mom was a happier thing to do rather than participating in the plethora of activities. Gradually she engrossed Suryansh and looked towards where all the adults were sitting. Here on the veranda, at quite a height from the ground, she saw all the females sitting in Burqa and now became conscious of her sleeveless blue top with bead work and skin-coloured capris.

One was so used to dressing scantily in this country for outings. Suryansh's decibel level was now higher than the general atmosphere. Ria wasn't in particular invited on the veranda and after a little contemplation, decided to let Suryansh enjoy the activities and stay with him rather than say a goodbye to the party.

There was sweet little Ayesha sitting in a corner of the table with two other kids and a grown-up boy, a cousin paying them attention and making her laugh heartily. By now Suryansh had his naughty smile settled on his face and he rushed to the large chocolate fondue fountain. Here the Sheikh, father of Ayesha, spoke very lovingly to Suryansh.

When the kid wanted to use the restroom, they were directed to one of the villas. Grandeur and opulence dictated the high-ceilinged villa. On the right side of the enormous washroom was a living room for children. Two dozen or so orange and pink and blue coloured single seat small sofas, in the shape of a hand, lined the room around a traditional carpet. That was the kid's living room. Most of the décor was glitzy and she could see state of the art elevators with real gold fringes.

Come spring and it was also Suryansh's birthday. This birthday had to be special for a boy always holding buzzing transport toys in his hands, marvelling at them, mimicking the sounds their real versions produced in the air, on the show windows, tables .It had to be with a big machine. A Hummer may be. She checked on the 'rent a car' outlet. The black hummer at one near Mega mall looked fantastic. The two brothers who owned the shop agreed on the rent with a smile after she cited the child's fascination for the machines. A child whose list of first few words in the vocabulary included con-crete mi-xer trrrruck.

Sumit became a party to the plan, found a rental, which also took care of the insurance even though being one and half times priced more. He had to play safe, Sumit style. On the day of the birthday, they reached the pick up place. It was a shining white Hummer, H3. The sheer volume of the space inside was majestic. Suryansh didn't take to the excitement instantly and held onto his toy tractor. His white Corolla was being left behind and the boy who literally grew up in that didn't quite fathom it. He was concerned. After being assured he began to notice the big machine. The excitement started building up a thrill for everyone. Driving this down on the sultry roads of the outskirts of the emirate was an experience in itself.

The brothers from the 'rent a car' called. "But then, only for your child we had reduced the price, got the vehicle washed and placed a small surprise for him inside".

Hummer with its controls, proportions and clearance was some driving experience. They went into the periphery of the dunes. When you move your ring finger slightly in the sun, squint your eyes and see those even 'low in carat' diamonds emitting tiny colour specs, one gets involved looking at the same. The child, the sand, the sun, the father with a camera, the big machine and a huge expanse of space, as far as you could look! All of them now tiny coloured glinting specs!

Sumit didn't want to venture into the dunes. That officially required a special license and skill. So when was Ria to try that then! The birthday had to continue. The accelerator of the Hummer was the best lever operated on by this driver and the need to speed, as visible with the localites now was understood by her. Well, the vacant smooth roads did provide an opportunity for the same and the Hummer's speed, nothing less than120 km/hr was music in itself.

Mother and son dropped dad to the office, next morning in the SAIF zone and went ahead to try on the machine in the magnanimous and enticing sands. Whoop! What fun at the tilts, sheer and play of torque. Another tilt and a scream from the child in the car seat in the back and Sumit's son held at an oblique angle. Couldn't risk or manage it further, Ria got out and opened up Suryansh's straps. They walked towards the road and Ria signalled for help. The next approaching vehicle stopped immediately and the driver took her keys and smoothly brought the Hummer onto the road.

On the wrong side of the genes inhabited, the scared child had a story now to tell everyone he knew. What an experience, being stuck at 45 degrees and then documenting the mini-rescue through her camera, Ria had her fill of an adventure.

Atmosphere around was changing. The market had a hushed tone. There were mixed reviews about the inflow of work everywhere. Sabah's stories moved to imparting traditional wisdom that survives it all. Patience! And laughter and playing with children with whom there was no shared language. He spoke about the importance of having female friends (also sighing now for a granddaughter) that kept everyone cared for, loved and imparts targets for men.

"A cargo plane crashed right in front of my eyes this afternoon" shared Sumit. But the topic of discussion was the same as the discord of the previous evenings since a fortnight.

Next day she read about the incident on the front page of Khaleej times and shuddered at the enormity of the situation. It was a shocker in the face. Now scared, she called up Sumit. They both needed the assurances of a normalcy, the kind a routine of the house brings.

The image from the aerobatic display printed on a glossy sheet was in her hand to take home for the kid. That of an MIG selected for a publication. That of an MIG and my pictures of the trucks in the sand came out in print on a glazed paper.

There were few more in print. The shadows on the tracks of monster trucks and of human shadows marring the footprints of camels. The black watering pipes feeding the entire stretch, testimonial to the human effort of making the road shoulder green.

The same sand reflected in the lower foliage of palms and top layers of green, which looked especially astounding on the wavy road. The trick was to follow the zooming car, which knew the location of a camera and to raise the volume in order to combat the 120-beeping sound.

After being thrown out of the library, the excursions shifted to the other side of the road, to the open piazza with the child running around and shouting on the endless pavers and redrawing patterns of the white streaks of the planes in the sky with his tiny hands outstretched towards them in the air. Suryansh needed to find a friend that he could regularly meet outside.

CHAPTER 14

Muse

The weather going turbulent makes the scene only more reddish and heightens my feelings, like the contrast of the rose called Anvil Sparks. My excitement builds up at the sense of togetherness. The touch grows warmer. Out the plane comes, leaving contrails behind. Now the night reflects on the clouds below- the best hues, the colour grey has to offer and I am ready to step out of the window.

Lights going live and the announcements bring you back to the modalities, now only the warm touch of the hand as a gentle reminder and the constant communicator.

If I touch my fingers myself, remembering the intensity when you held them, I get that same electric current in my body.

Baffled by the dream Ria woke up.

Abhiyansh:

I wake myself up in the night to relive and memorise-feel each pearl, put in the string again. I rehearsed the touch, the feel, the sounds, and the words spoken. Those make me numb but my heart reacts. It exudes a thrilling wave of passion and a deep smile in mind.

Transformed, I was after having returned from the war photography with my love requited by Aica. And how humane and thankful I was. Contentment gives a timeless twinkle to the eye.

"You look like a Goddess with natural light falling on you from the side, your skin is shining, the neck bones are contouring the shadows so well. The complexion is well contrasted." I had said after asking if I could describe her to her.

And then touched her everywhere with closed eyes. "I can sculpt you now. "

I clicked her without any hindrances of fabrics. She was relaxed and my camera relied on her.

With her arm up, the soft weaves of her hair in the background and the late afternoon light sculpting her before I did, I got to click her perfectly formed curvatures of the neck and shoulder, her sides, the inside curvatures of her breast and tantalizing smooth curve of her waist before the light softened.

And her back! Damn charming in the soft light. She could arch like how only ballerinas and flamingos can. After the shot, I came close and slid my arm across the waist slowly, gliding from the small of the back to the side. She overlaid her hand on mine and moved it up as if prodding to break into a dance together. Well, a dance together it was, me inside her, a synchronized movement of vitality and craving.

She was more important to me than work. Aica was aware of the charm she, as a woman, held over men. Those eyes were enough to kill and make a man go weak in his knees. People were in awe of her grace. Strengthening exercises not only did her body good, they strengthened her to a completely serenading persona tuned to the music of the Nutcracker.

When what you want and what is right is at odds with each other, she could make people surrender with her charm alone. And if she weaved a web of words, with its waves and syntax, spread out like an art form of peach-coloured ballet shoe ribbons in a circular room. You could bend your knees and get under it or hold the fragile network with your arms under it. But one couldn't cross through it.

I wanted to make love to her like she had never been loved before.

Abhiyansh again:

The proportions and smoothness, if I had clicked Ria, I would have definitely got turned on. Otherwise, my entire team was professional at clicking nudes. But it was my work. When she lifted herself to put the stuff on the upper shelf- the curve of her waist revealed itself to me and I was awestruck. I couldn't move and my mind didn't work further. Only if I had asked, even if she had said no, I could click her. Her shoulders were my zooming destination, tantalizing. If this wish could be a reality! But then she was way too young and naive. Maybe she would have taken it otherwise and not understood the poetic intent.

In the gallery, some pictures were without a caption. You looked into the image with your own perception. That went with an instant liking.

I did the same. The captions and the stories behind were on pull-outs for those who wanted to know the photographer's perception or concept of the frame.

I could not give out the caption of my intent to her by myself.

*****

I should stop looking for that Idol experience in love.

For "He" is the one. We smile in tandem.

For you and with you alone, I feel in harmony

Aica sneaked him into the dressing room and he could make chic images out of the flurry of activity in there before being sent out. With tutus fluttering and hands moving swiftly with make–up, it was difficult to position onself without being conspicuous. He wondered how the painter Edgar Degas could have spent hours in the dancing class in the eighteenth century producing a movement of colour and charming details on canvas. Like the illusions created in the paintings, he challenged himself to produce illusions with his work of art.

Aica never had inhibitions. For us it wasn't only physical, it was the minds. So, what was to hide and what was in it, to not give in to!

She was the lemon English rose, Graham Thomas In its fullness, yet fragile and slightly fragrant, smelling only to those who held the suave petals closer and breathed them deeply.

For Aica:

I am shouting at everyone, my patience is done, you have disturbed my harmony, my head aches and my heart aches. I want peace and solitude. More than anything, I want you. I want you to smile and hold me, hold me in your arms and tell me its all good. Take me in you and keep me there, held in you, a part of you. When you give yourself too much into someone else's complications, on them being solved, you are left standing alone. You are pained for somebody else's pain. A safe distance, forgotten on the way. It wasn't about the frequency; it was about the intention.

Years later, for Ria:

The pain is the same again. I am not shouting at anyone, I am patient. My harmony is disturbed, my head hurts, and my heartaches. I know I will get over this and reach peace in solitude. I am holding you and you are a part of me.

Can we smile again and get back the spring in our heart, lightness in our spirit.

*****

Abhiyansh completed reading Aica's mail:

"I want to teach you no more.... I thought the teaching and standing by you would help you overcome your turbulence. When in a relationship one person alters and doesn't reform, the other person writhes. I had let the whole stuff be apparent.

I lived your life; I stepped up with you to understand. I am going to retract now. I loved you more than anyone. There is no God on earth that you seek.....only bits of HIM in people. Why did you seek that?

The moment is now. The rules are for an arrangement. Arrangement with a commitment- for the unknown measures of time! Ironical it is, people make rules for being in love....to carry it further.....

Love is spontaneous, doesn't require effort, rules or long words."

*****

In my need to be inspired, to share and care, Ria had started becoming my fanciful escape from the grind.

If her fragrance could be bottled at the source.

Till you didn't know you were in the process of owning my heart,

It was all spontaneous, the most beautiful.

My plate is full. It will be painful to let you go. I am scared to keep you in bits.

What if the camera in her hand could be me?

We human beings have a problem. When we are too happy we do not flow- we try to restrain or hold on to some kind of sadness, ethics, time or any other factor and ruin it for ourselves. It almost rained today when I thought of her.

More than the perspective visible in the photograph, it was about the perspective of the person behind the shutter and later the perspective of the person in front of the print gazing at it. And how much of space was wanted in between. What you clicked was as important as what you camouflaged. The surroundings of the frame captured could actually be in complete contrast to it.

But such people always give you something and go, said Negi.

The picturesque roads of the long drive had all become silent to him when Aica had left. He gained more wisdom to himself and had become a deeper person though but the recklessness didn't quite catch up.

Ria:

Mixing her yoga with dance she could see the slight bulge of belly, twisted toes and stretched upper side of legs. She wanted a camera installed in her own eyes to capture that for her screen.

Awareness as the key, you could lose the thrill of a game once you decipher the codes. She kept recognising and making sense of it. Not a need, it was a want.

What and why were also important to me. Sometimes the answer came very late and you could be thrown out of your sensibilities.

If only Ria could get herself clicked by Abhiyansh. Sumit clicked her after dishearteningly agreeing. The artistic expression was missing in the pictures. They did not match with what she saw about herself in the mirror. The toning was captured well but the erotic art fled completely. Now she wished she could install a camera in the mirrors of her bedroom. The sensuousness that she experienced was worth catching in her lithe frame.

A sense; inappropriate or beyond perceivable, but powerful and strange, becoming of you.

CHAPTER 15

Continuum

Sabah asked Ria to take over his studio for the client facing completely. His son, a student, was a few years away from taking over. Her credentials were to be attested in the UAE embassy, New Delhi. That gave Suryansh a chance to witness the festival of Diwali in India, which was as full of love as Eid, only more colourful in the night sky. And meanwhile, Sumit re-visited London. Returning home was splendid as always after Sumit's travel abroad. The dining table was full of gifts. It seemed like he had forgotten to get anything for himself.

In the evening Ria and Suryansh walked to the office carrying Indian mithai and planning to add another gadget to Sumit's collection as a surprise. Eid was around the corner and it seemed the fervour of Diwali in India had just continued for them. Sabah saw them walking towards his cabin, exclaimed with a loud welcoming cheer to whosoever he was speaking to over the phone "Oh! My daughter is here". This was etched in her echoic memory forever. George, Abraham and Zia, Khalid's welcoming effervescence was equated by Suryansh. He then sat with her as she switched on her computer. Her chair hurt his hand. The child looked angrily at her and tears formed in his eyes but he didn't make a noise, to maintain the sanctity of her office. Sabah bade him goodbye with Eidi in his little hands.

The local markets were usually abuzz till 11 in the night and there was no hurry in the morning. With Eid around the corner, the same extended to the malls, public places and the air was brightened with celebratory lights everywhere.

Few sips of pina colada and the smoked beer from his glass got her into focusing on the immediate. All she was conscious of was the wall and Sumit. The piano in the background wasn't playing to her understanding.

Ria didn't like the pina colada. Ajman it was, at such a close distance, unfrequented by them all this time. Now they had the whole bar/ restaurant to themselves, with just an old couple dancing to the piano and adding such charm to the evening. The piano wasn't the live piano, it was a silent one. And how come the light was dancing in harmony with the ol' jiggly-wigglies in such a slow motion. The second replacement had also tasted of sour coconut. This time the bartender came over, apologized and probed into the matter.

Isn't it a mocktail?

Didn't you order a cocktail Mam?

So, she had her taste of alcohol. Sumit had never given to her fondness for taking things up to the level of obsession. She on her own hadn't ventured on the path of stimulants. Now knowing that she had consumed alcohol, she got the tipsiness, enjoyed the evening and tried to be tipsier in order to feel the full effect. Sumit got concerned and wanted to hire a taxi. They could come for the car the next day. But now Mademoiselle was walking with an induced expression, to and fro in the hotel lobby and wouldn't give her car away for anything.

The whispering in the air was that no new contracts had been bagged in the last month. Sabah assigned some documenting assignments, similar one after the other in a row, which left Ria in exasperation over the next month. Never afraid to express herself, she mentioned the same to him. Post the office hours, he called her on his way home and in a minimum of words imparted that he didn't want Ria to lose her job and was making up those assignments. Otherwise, there was no work in the market.

Dubai mall had opened up and again boasted of world-class features. Suryansh danced in front of the magnanimous feature and then looked excitedly at the animals in the zoo section. And what was that!

It was unbelievable. Those were real penguins in the Middle East. Suryansh ran towards them, flapping his arms and Sumit got perplexed by the cruelty of man. What were these people with money doing, at whim bringing anyone at their disposal? Penguins! The importance of maintaining the ecosystem, tradition and diversity rang in Ria's head.

The news of her husband's remarriage broke Mumtaz. He reasoned it with his long wait! Her children were now at the grandmother's place. The elder son was especially disoriented. Mumtaz did not turn up for a few days. Her grace, promptness, agility of body, youth faded. Also, she became curt and spoke the bare minimum. One weekend she asked if Ria wanted to catch up on missed sleep, took the child out to play, shutting the door politely behind.

Later as Mumtaz rushed to attend to Suryansh's boiling milk, the message beeping on Ria's mobile read that five Dhs had been transferred to a number. Was it possible to transfer money like that? The benefactor's number belonged to Mumtaz. Ria's phone had been outside. She asked her why the message and Mumtaz sounded just as surprised. The house had no locks in any of the cupboards. She and Sumit discussed this for the first time. How this one bit of news had changed the life of this woman. Quickly her hair started greying, the body started losing its fitness. Always irritated and strained, one day she fought. Employment revoked; she left the house with the Gulf Times supplement. Furious, Ria said she couldn't take anything from the house, not even the meagre supplement with advertisements for help required at homes. She spoke also about the money transfers, which she had let go of.

Ria was troubled, it wasn't a help that left her house but also a companion, she had got used to and cared for. They both had raised Suryansh together in harmonious days. She had taken care of Ria too. Without her, raising up the little boy would have been a work instead of the pleasure that the three in each other's company had made it out to be.

While Ria was taking an untimely coffee break in the office, a call from Sumit confirmed the rumour that his office was shutting down its operations in Sharjah and shifting to south India next year, to cut down on costs and to keep afloat in the economic ruckus. The dirhams to INR conversion of the salary wouldn't be proportional and the major salary cut was impending over a month's time.

They were to shift to an apartment in the building on the way to the art area. After the initial shock subsided, Ria gained her composure and knew that they would find a way or the other to hold on there. With all the pieces fitting together, it couldn't alter now just like that, in her belief. They would survive the pitfall.

They continued with their decorum of lifestyle as always, with the necessary changes reckoned with.

Ria met Mumtaz at the building entrance sometimes, the apartment they had shifted to, again company provided.

Life is a changeable fiction. And there was a whole year to work things out. The Ethiopian help came wearing a long skirt, a pleated top, crisp curly mop of hair, dyed bronze. She showed her labour card, which was valid. They decided on a salary and she was to start from the next day.

Next morning she turned up looking very crisp again. When Ria opened the door, she became a little conscious of her own night suit and haggard sleepy look. Dema quickly changed into work clothes. She went to the market and got groceries, cooked a fabulous gravy in red tomatoes.

That worked well with her. Only the rotis, if they were lucky, they could eat. Soon she found a job at an Internet café and employed her very pleasant looking cousin who couldn't converse in English. How love needed no language, was a sight to behold. Which language did she and Suryansh implicate, Ria never understood. Only she could hear laughter from the next room. How wonderfully could she make a child squeal, whatever was the communication and the bond of friendship.

Work, or the made-up work at the office consumed Ria's morning hours. Now she knew why the local aunties in order to pass their time refilled Sheesha while constantly eating seeds, one by one, all kinds of them, from sunflower to wasabi.

But perpetual was the thought of staying back somehow, with Sumit's search for a new job getting worked out.

CHAPTER 16

The fall

The fall of Nasdaq, Dow Jones, Nikkei, Sensex…..the action on Wall Street. How could the waves be without disturbance?

Dubai was on fire! People were fleeing. Fleeing to insecurity, even if returning to their home countries. There was tension suspended in the still air. Everywhere you went, you could see the difference-traffic was getting a notch under on the roads. People spoke only of the economic downturn.

Nasdaq, Dow Jones, Nikkei were only falling … that was the first Ria had read about and it wasn't exciting anymore! There was a multitude of cars acquired on loan, now abandoned near the airport by fleeing expats. And a substantial increase in the advertisements for resale of vehicles, of all kinds. The placement newspaper started getting thinner day by day.

The weekends arrived in the same intervals but the light-heartedness was coming apart. The family did not return home from the excursions happy and satisfied. Son started asking" Mom where is Dubai submerging in water?" The couple realized they had to stop discussing their worries with him. But the "we" was also dissolving somewhere in the submerging Dubai. Both Ria and Sumit were in their troubled worlds. Acceptance of what was to be in the future was annoyingly confused.

The air wasn't palpable. The ambiguity was uncomfortable to withstand, especially with the media.

Also, discussions about office operations in the failing economy in the base country at an alarming rate started flying soon amongst the colleague community. Only one vertical, Oil and Gas was to be retained. The move for the rest was to supervene in about eight months' time. The job search became frantic in any of the Emirates or any of the other select countries.

Then came Nazma who was the opposite of Mumtaz simple in behaviour, full of humility and shy in nature. She seldom spoke. Sleep deprivation in the last house with otherwise good employers was the reason for the change.

In order to pass her time, she read The Quran. Sumit got a printed copy for her. Also, Ria let her work in Sudhaji's house on alternate days an hour each for extra money. She hardly knew anyone and would go out on Friday afternoons, dressed neatly and simply. Suryansh's laughter on watching Mr Bean and she would keep commenting it as dumb. "How is it made" was the next thing she liked to watch with Ria if Sumit was off to the club and Suryansh was sleeping.

Her taking over the house was a relief and Ria concentrated a full day on working out possibilities.

Like the seven ages of man...each playing a role...each role to be played.

In this strenuous scenario, Ria happened to find a morning friend- an old chap who would be waiting on the road at the junction. Ria spotted him when she went to see Suryansh off on the school bus. It had started with retaliation to the old gentleman's smiles and crisp salutations. And also, that he was able to smile and radiate energy early morning, he said he combined his meditation with a sleep of six hours.

The other morning, he was carrying a briefcase in one hand as usual and rolled blueprints of mechanical drawings in the crevice of his arm. He turned out to be a bigwig of the same industry as that of Sumit. Subimal Paul seemed impressed with Sumit's position, the reputation of the firm he worked for and spoke rapidly about the project he was overseeing- an upcoming airport, while his driver got the car. Subimal Paul asked for Sumit's CV while hastily settling in the car so as not to cause any disruption in the flow of traffic.

Going back to India was still months away. There had to be a reason for this meeting, she diligently got the resume the next morning. She couldn't relax now, the work in her own office diminished and she quit. There was no point in going to the office and work on fake assignments and add to the running cost of struggling Sabah's office. Now she spent her entire time searching for his job.

Discussion of the state of affairs was palpable in homes, supermarkets and on pavements. Soon the hype around the world's tallest tower Burj Dubai too started fleeting in the air. The monument of excesses reaching out to the sky seemed to be in a dilemma itself. A true representation of the status quo!

The deregulation after the Depression was now taking its toll on the child and the man in front of her eyes, running on the sand on a weekend - the man wearing a worried expression but playing with the child and the child, not oblivious of the stress on the father's face. The traffic on the roads had dwindled. Everywhere people spoke of the bursting of the bubble. Suryansh in the park overheard about the drowning of Dubai and came inquiring about the flooding waters again and of bubbles bursting but not bringing pleasure to the crazy adults, the crisis of course not comprehensible to him.

The Gulf News was thinning further, losing content and weight day by day. The number of pages in the job section lessened to four, from the huge pile it used to be. The cars supplement was the only one, which retained its bulk, used cars were heftily on sale. Suryansh kept on cutting their pictures and adding them to his scrap album. The fourth estate again in general didn't talk much about the hue and cry and maintained decorum of the opinion sections about the world with the same enthusiasm.

In the general atmosphere outside you could sense it but not know about it. Only much later did it summarise to paying for de-regulation, laundering of money by financial firms and playing around with their books. What Ria gathered from beating her head in all kinds of discussions with friends abroad, reading, watching was that, somewhere in the banks of Iceland and the like, a lot of money was fabricated and used to mount house prices and speculate on financial markets.

While the folks went about their regular stuff without worrying an iota about the rock-solid housing financial market on which the economy of the US stood tall and every perceivable plot as seen by a satellite in Dubai and Abu Dhabi, which could have a skyscraper was either seen in construction or in the pipeline. There were some number giants racking their heads.

As learnt years later, these number giants, fund managers and investors who were witnessing the mortgage market crash as speculated by them earlier had made whooping billions out of their betting. But then this was trade for these sniffers, using unregulated derivatives as financial invasion, gambling on anything, even weather. Whose fault was the collapse? Of the banks, global financial service firms, security management firms, rating agencies, the government who were to regulate the industry or whom?

Collapsing at the weakest link, the housing finance market initiated the waves for the downtrend of economics, which was to affect many, UAE too being at the hulk of the tornado. Common people knew they couldn't be bailed out, like the huge banks. The robust economies like Iceland were collapsing. After hastily losing their jobs and businesses, the expats left with whatever was left and fled to their home countries in equal pronto. So the airports were full of abandoned cars, all of them on loans - which was no use paying now.

The scurried movement all around was palpable now and month after month the dilemma continued. The epitome of luxury, Burj Dubai, a projection to the future, which could be promising, only that it was in debt now.

Ria left out no office listed and no contact, which she could not use. There was no need to go back if they kept at the search. She simply could not go back. The air in the house was also getting as palpably strained as much as it was outside. March would be approaching in four long months.

The announcement of the opening up of Burj Dubai was made official. Only, it was unveiled as Burj Khalifa, after the ruler of Abu Dhabi Sheikh Khalifa bin Zayed al-Nahayan, head of the United Arab Emirates who rescued his neighbouring debt-laden emirate. Over tea in Sudhaji's balcony in Sharjah, with the revealing of official height and spraying of fantastic well-coordinated fireworks, Ria and Suryansh witnessed it, facilitated by the clear skies of Sharjah and Dubai in the first week of January.

Next morning, the newspaper carried a glossy poster of Burj Khalifa, the icon of neo-futurism. And nothing still, about the global financial recession! The ostentatious tower boasting of 200 storeys, 828m above ground and an enormous view from the observation deck and Avant-garde styling, with one-fourth of its height non-useable and only to soar higher than any other building yet, seemed to be a metaphor of exuberant mockery.

Suryansh heard about their 'going back' from Sudhaji. She had taken the toy-fascinated child to a store for a farewell gift. The child told the aunt, who was a partner in crime, that he did not want lots of toys, only one of the real Maserati to take back to India. Sudhaji expressed her incompetence at buying the real car and offered to buy a lottery ticket instead. The child came home with toys and a Mashreq lottery ticket.

This was the final month before leaving the house and it was stifling. One hour started getting to be the calmest one in her strained day. That was the one spent in the art area painting class. The evenings brightened up the courtyard with the birds very welcoming. She would walk to the art area. The people in the art area recognized her, having seen her with a camera and later with Suryansh so often. Now she regretted and tried to retrace in thought why joining the painting classes never occurred to her in all these years.

The ether was very cordial and creative still. The commercial angle of the establishment didn't exist beyond the nominal fees. The Iranian master was of a congenial temperament and educated them well. He also taught about the evolution of various movements and the journey towards post modernism. Many women brought their work, which were rhythmic renditions of their holy book or Arabic alphabets in calligraphy. For rest of the work, the teacher instructed, was to be depictive and not realistic a representation. Of mermaids and forms. One young girl was so fond of dinosaurs; her work had dinosaurs going about their daily activities in her house.

Also, she now submitted her entry to the photography museum. The desert series she had undertaken before joining Sabah's office was now in large prints at the desk of the Director's office.

Suryansh also accompanied her sometimes. Ashraf duly gave him art supplies. The Iranian teacher suggested if she could paint something with a reflection from her country of origin. It was to be a pleasing representation only. A Rajasthani woman with an oversized pot on her head, drawn in the major space and three-square traditional motifs on the side came up on the canvas. It was her first attempt at drawing human forms. The arm came up at a rather abrupt angle, the one holding the pot. Master made no attempt to make her redraw the form. Symbolism, he said, just go ahead.

It showed her right profile mostly, head covered and duppatta trailing, complete with ornaments and a dot on the forehead. The wheatish skin and the clothes painted bright orange, yellow, hints of red. The face got a smudge of paint from Ria's hand the next day and the repairing job that she attempted was making it worse. The Iranian master came to the rescue and assured that he would repair the face but with a puzzled expression he pointed at the belly of the woman. "What is to be done here?" He enquired. He couldn't make out any sense from the skin tone on the belly. On being described that the belly remains uncovered, the guy showed confused reactions. The painting was complete but the face stain botched up was making Ria restless.

That evening Suryansh had also accompanied her to the class. He was made to feel welcome and given some more art supplies than usual by Ashraf. Ria approached the master sitting in the courtyard by the dark evening with his colleagues, enjoying chitchat. The courtyard looked homey; a pang of non- belonging here appeared. He amusedly asked why couldn't she wait for him instead of her second attempt at repairing the poor lady's face with lovely finery and clothes and adding a very irritating scar on the cheek. He mixed colours on the palette and profusely merged the scar like an expert plastic surgeon, did not add detail or shadows, just repaired the damage that the painter's restlessness had incurred.

As the realization of going back sank in eventually with the return dates and tickets, the 'to-do' list emerged. Egypt which could have been any weekend, Oman, which was at a drivable distance and the Corolla had come with a visa offer. A voucher for the stay in the desert tents was still unused. A stay in the Madinat Jumeirah which was planned for the anniversary was pending.

The list changed to what was practically possible now in fifteen days, which was very different. Also, Suryansh had few cards with a big balance in the play areas and the following days included that along with necessary jobs.

The living room without the red sofa now sold off was a reminder of a span gone by. It was painful, expressed by both Nazma and Ria. Sumit was stoic and going about the arrangements, one by one.

The last drive of the white Corolla was to the car assessment authority where Zahra's husband worked. It was a single hand, lady driven car, which fetched good money and was going to Africa.

Ria as always removed her favourite sandals before driving. Therapeutic that driving was for her, habitually a tinker of two things at a time. Driving kind of suited her very well. Like one part of the brain was driving and the other one was thinking with maximum concentration. And when she drove at a good speed, she did only one thing at a time with full consciousness. It was thrilling, meditative almost- a drive like that always energized her, gave her the inertia. How you make a game challenging for yourself and then play with full interest.

The last drive on the white Corolla with the number plate of Sharjah, Sumit commented something about Ria's driving. That was so unexpected and it initiated a furious reaction from Ria who was viewing it emotionally and was probably hoping for an understanding or expression of the same. On the contrary, hearing instructions from a person in the passenger seat mentally driving the car infuriated her. Not a red slip in the entire span of driving in that country and someone commenting even on her last ride.

Sumit hardly bought any stuff for himself. He had mentioned a few times about the i-Phone. Everyone was taking back a new LCD, otherwise Sumit hadn't shopped for almost a year. Finishing off the balance from old cards in the gaming areas of Mega mall was a great evening. At the i-Phone kiosk, they enquired about the phone. 3Gs was the recent launch. The salesman said he had twelve of them for a Sheikh who would be arriving any minute.

Ria and Sumit bargained for one. Sumit gave up as the salesman didn't budge but Ria was determined because there wasn't much time left and once this chance was gone, who knew what. On persisting, the salesman did agree to part with one piece out of the dozen he held. The duo had a winning smile, knowing that the new gadget would be used dearly.

The return flight was the next day. The stuff was sold or shipped back. The last evening was a pleasant one in a long long time, all said and unsaid, done with. Suryansh was scared of ants; he was seeing them for the first time. And some entertainment it was for the parents to see him squeal merrily at the roar of lion at the zoo. So at least there was something he was scared of.

Nazma was to be sent off to Poornima's house with the double blanket and gold chain for her little daughter the next day as they left for the airport. Sumit's walking to Lulu to buy the gold chain and giving it to Nazma sitting on the leftover piece of furniture, her surprise and happy acceptance of it was the most satisfying spectre in a million days gone by.

You have to feel happy going back home. If you do not feel that, something has to be altered at home. Alter it, work on it, till you start feeling happy going home. Coaxing herself into this, she boarded.

Her personal heaven vanished in the matter of a single international flight.

A clock, deep blue, rectangular, with falcons printed, Ria remembered now in the aircraft, was left behind, hanging above the mirror in their bedroom.

CHAPTER 17

Return

You know yourself after the journey.

There was no time to introspect. All that it was, a slow unwinding shock!

At the IGI, New Delhi, a bystander saw her with a pram, a wailing child, a luggage trolley and kept checking her out. She stared back and asked if he would like to help. Parents had sold off their house and retired to an ashram in Pune. The van arranged for them graciously by a friend carried their big suitcases. When Suryansh woke up it was a jumpy van, which wasn't driving in any lane in a dim-lit city. And the steering was on the wrong side.

Was it a going back to India or coming back! It definitely was coming behind times. And in some sense, also returning to a full circle, to the point, where having been in the very first place had prompted to look out for progress.

Delhi was a transformed place. There was lesser honking on the roads but the road rush, rashness and absurdity had increased multifolds. An apartment had to be rented in Gurgaon in a jiffy because the possession of the apartment booked in a housing society was held back by the builder. It was being used for ancillary purposes as it had belonged to NRIs.

The temperature plummeted to 48 degrees Celsius that summer. And Suryansh remained unwell throughout. Sudhaji called to share that her entire stuff was lost in transit.

Money brought back was dwindling fast. In buying two cars, since Gurgaon had limited movement without one, this and those fees and settlements and other unprecedented expenses. Everybody seemed crazed for money without respect for time and professionalism. A service guy would confirm the pickup time at one and unapologetically turn up at four. Even the colony's mali was after your money rather than being bothered about the plants.

Why was everyone just selling? You couldn't hold a decent conversation even with the mali. He wanted to sell you the mitti, khad, planter and also a small sachet of something, an activator perhaps to make the khad work. It was endless. The juicewalla was more interested in other stuff than offering you a minute and a tissue box. Everyone seemed time-bound in earning money from the banker to the guard. There was endless haggling about the money everywhere.

The mobile constantly beeped with messages and calls in the afternoon, should one try to catch a wink of peaceful sleep along with the sick child. These were from people who wanted to sell you something or the other, who wanted to keep a tab on how you were investing your money –they could always offer better options. If nothing else, the girl at the other end wanted you to send your dry-cleaning stuff to her employer, the one who most likely hired her for her meek look and a feminine voice. Some calls were even from unknown places with full information about your child.

Their stuff arrived with some causality. How many cartons of toys had they got back in a small apartment! Now Ria simply could not breathe. Whether to dismantle stuff or to wait for the possession of the apartment go to the court or tussle with other options. The room full of toys started getting trampled on soon and dusty. Dust on toys? Were they to dust the toys and then play, never had they imagined. Living in that house with half-open cartons became a daily struggle.

Even late in the evening, Suryansh in the green spaces in the housing colony kept feeling sick. The paediatrician advised him to stay in air-conditioned environment all the time to acclimatise. After an argument that lasted four days, about whether a new conditioner was to be bought in the rented apartment or wait for moving into the new apartment, which would have one, installed in each room, it was bought.

The toys had to be cleaned every time Suryansh wanted to play. The stacked racks too lost their crispness in the transit and reassembling, the toy room started becoming a junkie place. To put out so many toys out on display on the racks in the toy room became a difficult task and they too started getting damaged. The unseen challenges, that too mundane ones and seeing to a sick kid, Ria was left with no mind space for any kind of relaxation, let aside the creative satisfaction.

The weekends were no longer weekends. They were just a continuity of struggled existence and grind of the week. The extended families were away now. Friends had moved on to their growth in careers and building up their place in the hierarchy of society. Whatever had happened to the simplicity of friendship?

We had to build it again; not having come back to something was her reflection. But where was the time and energy to connect to being "we" and us? She was wasted in emotional upheaval and he was consumed in his career or maybe in something else, she didn't even have an inkling.

Sumit was seeking his own bearings. When he had left the country, it was his life alone. Now in the same country, there was a family with him and he had no grip. Planning in distress did not come naturally to him and the house was too unsettled, too troublesome. A home as in a "home" was muffled. And Big Bazaar was a crude form to Carrefour as Carrefour was to Sainsbury. Sumit had so many challenges in his job; his was a return to an unorganized work culture. 'People in offices speak more and act less, here' is all he said, not wanting to discuss his routine.

There were always loads of challenges in the apartment, stuff brought back to assemble, a thousand chores waiting for him. And so much of fatigue! He said the child could very well go to a government school instead of the fancy international schools in Gurgaon, given the other big challenge.

Ria couldn't leave the sick child and go outside. Sitting in front of the desktop and searching for his job abroad became her little hope again. Maybe if they could go back to their old lives!

The wheels on road were frustrating. You came to buy groceries two km from your home, battered down by the bus suddenly decelerating to zero on a speed breaker the size of a mountain. The child on board sticker on the car was so out of context here, back home. In fact, after a few days the sticker became dirty and a foolish reminder of a different system elsewhere. Also, what would you be considerate about- a particular baby in yet another car in front, when the whole of India was so full of babies, everywhere you looked.

Better consideration than the sticker went in convincing the beggar on the road not to use her three-month-old as a bait for begging even in the harsh summer months.

From the stance of 'never to fight' to 'fighting was also ok' was a quick move. What is important is what type of fights you pick. More important than that is how you close the fights. How easy it was earlier when in the end, both were lightened and there are smiles and hugs!

On resumed the old weekend regime. The closest place of interest seemed to be the Apparel house, Epicentre. Frustration began from the parking itself. There was no event going on and the restaurant was totally empty. She tried to enrol for a painting class. Ms Vandy Talwar's classes on the premises itself was found to be a possibility. A discussion with the artist over the telephone, the strong smell of commercials around it and logistics did not seem to be working out.

Friends had moved to the lifestyle of brands and adapting to the mall culture, so many of which had sprung up in Gurgaon, most of them very small in size and with limited outlets. The next few weekends were attempts again to catch up with them, mostly futile. The child could not stand the temperature outside, which that year was on a record extreme and most of the air-conditioned malls of Gurgaon were too small and all were crowded. The mall with a big bookstore did not have outlets for groceries or clothes or entertainment. For a list of all three of them, different malls had to be visited. It was a run, run game. And in weekdays, by the time Sumit returned from his office, took a breather and got ready for the market, it would be closed.

Sumit squeezed a day out and they thought of showing around a glimpse of the capital to the kid and took him to Connaught place, their favourite. It was all dug up in the preparation of the Common Wealth Games. Dug up badly everywhere and everyone in Delhi was angry about their taxes lost in CWG scams. And such a prestigious event being organised in an ironically unorganised way! The preparation was not undertaken till the red flag blew and then everything screwed up. Gone were the thick pipes one sat on in front of Wenger's and walking around the colonnaded verandas was more of a challenge than a pleasure.

In the inner circle, Suryansh looked on hopefully for play areas and large swings. There were none and he couldn't make sense of lavish greens without such an activity. The National Art Museum turned out to be very hot without the air conditioning on and he had to take off his T-shirt. Driving through with the President's house on the right, he said it was a huge building, standing up in the back seat, broadening his shoulders and said that he liked slender and tall buildings. Enough of this excursion, they went back home to watch TV. The cartoon channels with million ads jutted in.

Suryansh had to be taught to refuse eatables offered by anyone out of the home. He gave a perplexed look even though his friendliness didn't change much. He would end up striking conversations with chosen strangers now. Maybe his skills at judging people sharpened too.

The desert pictures, Amro wrote in LinkedIn messages, were put up in the exhibition, inaugurated by the Sheikh and another highlight was her painting. Ria was stunned, knowing fully well what a painter she was, without any technique or experience. This time when she would go back, she would definitely do something with that form of art, may be work out opening a gallery or associate with one. She wanted to know more but Amro didn't reply further and then life happened and it blurred out.

The sales in the malls were unauthentic. He just did not like going to the malls too- they were over crowded, the jhulas weren't half as good as he was used to. Suryansh said the chicken nuggets he was used to at the same outlets back home were different here, they were deep-fried.

Exiting the lift after being stuck for forty-five minutes and shocked by claustrophobia, she jumped out. A fractured foot condemned her to limited movement.

By the time they moved to their own house in Gurgaon bought only as an investment earlier, they had no financial resources left to mould it into a presentable, liveable home. The builder in Gurgaon had sold them a half concrete-half sand dream. The apartment matched nowhere to the sample apartment in the quality of construction and specifications agreed upon. Mosquitoes bit them if the doors were left open. The plaster flaked on the walls. The windows had thin panes and the gaps between the doors and windows leaked air.

The child too had to be taught to shut the doors in the house because the AC was on. He soon lost his habit of keeping his room immaculate.

All that we had built on logic and their perception of how living could be, was fleeting away. Your belief and your treatment of it only turns a thing of no consequence into a thing of consequence. The stronger the belief, the higher the importance attached. Slowly a furrow started to appear on her forehead and on Sumit's too.

Night photography at Madinat Jumeirah and the water's images came out of a carton just opened and gave some encouragement. From the outdoor seating along the entire length of the promenade Sumit and she had sat on a fine evening looking at the abras and the serenaded views across. The villas were partly visible as if in hints between the trees, the dark otherwise enhanced by few down lighters and accentuated by the moon above.

Walking further ahead she had set her tripod. On both the sides of a dark space you could see two of their favourite buildings - Madinat Jumeirah and Burj Al Arab. There were traditional features of chattris and low construction on one side and structural expressionism on the other.

Another one was of the pale glow of the uplighters on the arches encompassing the columns and windows above, along the entire length of the symmetrical elevation of Qasba.

Profiled parapet of the building highlighted by the yellow orange blobs of the sky came through the blue of the entire expanse. Suryansh's favourite big Ferris wheel standing tall with its radiating arms and the cubicles looking as beads seating people with an air of vigour. Sigh!

Was it patience that had run out of relationships for everyone? Her son played when he could, in intermittent good health with the children of so many single moms in the park. Children talking far too much sense than hoped for. Why? What was so great about these effed up relationships and lost innocence.

"I bound myself to the vows, worked on them. It did not work out. I undid the vows and listened to the heart. In the hope that it could started working out." Ria sought help of people she could think of as sensible. A cousin told her to look at five good things in the spouse everyday for a week. Fighting till eternity was now easier. But it didn't seem right. What seemed right was to try working it out with complete sincerity.

The child was still not ready to tread onto the roads in autumn. There were no pavements or the pavements were completely broken ahead. And badly lit, if lit. Only the builder houses were lit well-hopelessly waiting for clients.

There were no light poles on the roads of Gurgaon and no light in Ria. She saw her child playing and looking towards her and was filled with guilt of not being able to participate cheerily in his play. This was killing, as if she could see the span of time passing by without having any control over it. Her movie, but she wasn't playing an active role in it. Surrounded by people, she was in her lonely self.

They all had shallow things to say which didn't feel like real conversations. She was unable to justify the role of a homemaker, mother, photographer and a wife.

Immediate deficit was the role of a wife - this she wanted to fill this in at the earliest. She saw her strength could come from the source of matrimony - since they had spent time as soul mates in belief. But he was troubled with her greys and could not connect to the sad her. This was adding on to the mess. If in the extremes of frustration for not being able to connect and derive energy from the relationship, which was nurtured with sweetness, it was turning hopeless – she screamed, screamed out in extreme ineptness, and spoke about revoking the marriage. He did the same.

To make do with much less of what he was making earlier, not coming back to a happy home. But he never spoke of it- not ready to ascertain that they were facing problems – somehow, he hoped things would turn on their own slowly and wanted them to understand and tried to behave normal.

These were not normal circumstances - to declare them so and work one by one step to clarify troubles or at least road mark the map was what she was arriving at. He could not distress further and accept or partner in it.

Nazma called to tell her, how she was perpetually beaten up by Poornima and was accused of stealing stuff including the double comforter Ria gave.

Already perplexed, news like this distressed the two of them. Now sitting in a different country what could they do to help the dumb, legally absconding Nazma.

The friends couldn't understand, the cribbing wasn't about returning to India only. It was about returning to the same troubles but with an exposure to a good life, burnt up patience in building that good life. And now to a stressed marriage!

Whatever happens to the personal happiness theory then? Why not be at peace then and make harmony the pursuit of "personal happiness." That is what started taking a toll on Ria the most. Aren't self-obsessed people better off without anchors? Weren't they mutual anchors? What of strong family bonds? Kids needed to thrive on it.

Yes, it was the expectation, which probably was the cause of all the trouble. Expectation of a normal time! Of those pleasant moments of friendship again, of small gestures which could make your breathing pattern normal. But if you left even this expectation completely, would any sustenance in the relationship really remain. So why not expect, value and be valued.

No money and lifestyle, no public places to go to on weekends and no emotional support from Sumit came to a horrible time. Going out with a child prone to sickness meant unable to work and unable to stay at home.

Those fluffy, delighted clouds popping up with mountains beyond when you look out of the oval pane. The clear formations, white frosted edges, and greyish blue on the inside. Those distant white buoyant ones merging with the soft blues. A smooth normal mind saw the blue sky contentedly merging itself with them.

The heavy dark clouds weighing down by the stuff they needed to drop. As the sky soared upwards without the clouds, it became deeper within itself, lost and ultramarine blue still higher above. Deeper blues of Ria, mixed with deepest of greys and with a flux.

The eyes refused to wear any shades and were lost, rather than looking.

All she needed was to expand herself, go beyond the physical limitations her body was bringing on and the plights of mind caused by interweaving or dependency in coarser terms with another being.

On the brighter side, awareness of art, alternate careers were picking up with the people at large. She started looking out.

The winters were unlit outside. Only the builder's houses lit, hopelessly waiting for customers in the mild recession that India was going through and not with full thrust.

The small balcony on the southern side did not accommodate them, just a washing machine. Watching her child playing happily, she was filled with guilt of not being able to participate in his play cheerfully. It was as if I could see my own life passing by and having no control over it. Surrounded by people, she was in her own lonely self. Felt like everyone had shallow things to say - there wasn't any real conversation.

When you grow past an anchor and the angelic you know that comes out of love.

She sensed that strength could be gained from the matrimony since the two had spent time as friends. Soul mates? Sumit was troubled too with her greys and the grind he had come back to. If in despair for not having been able to connect and derive energy, she screamed about revoking the marriage-he retaliated with fury. Later as they understood, she wanted to be held and told - all is going to be fine. He had his own struggles of settling down at work, make do with much less of what he was earning earlier, coming back to an unhappy home.

Aarija mailed her. She was going to Amsterdam to evaluate if she wanted to study there. That was the best news in ages. The two met at the airport for a short while and Ria returned with a pang from outside the departures.

Maybe, if they could go back to the old life together. Research on net, opinion of acquaintances, seniors, placed around and abroad opined if he studied further, his chances of getting a job could be ameliorated. In the humdrum, in order to talk that it could be done, it took ages to process since they could talk on weekends only.

Driving still frustrated her to no bounds. On a narrow road leading to the nearest market from her house, she would stop, get out and speak to the driver of the following car, sometimes cars for honking incessantly. Suryansh started refusing to go on a drive and complained of headache. One needed a driver for parking more than driving in NCR. And then you also needed a middleman to get you a good driver. This was an unorganized sector, upcoming of such agencies, many them non-registered with an authority.

How you hate being a third person for the two people in front of you. And equally, being non-existent for the single person in front of you. He said he hadn't been more far from life than in Sharjah. Didn't understand much but I feel it referred to lots of alcohol shops at each corner. In fact those were the landmarks in Gurgaon.

The efforts had to be put by themselves. To look at his positives for few days and report back to a cousin. She held on his cues, the ones he kept offering to a baffled her over phone.

When you both know each other so well and are put on a role where you just want to drop it and laugh-keep the masks away, of relationships, professions, situations that have been imposed on you or you have garbed yourself.

With her leg repaired and walking resumed she started venturing out. What to fill the emptiness with, if it can't be filled with work, relationships, and hobbies. New beliefs perhaps, then.

And faith- the little word with its expanse in multifolds. Butterflies and sunshine, beautiful and gratifying, yet a bit mysterious.

Gurgaon was full of guesthouses. They were dominated by the upcoming corporate culture. The sense of well-being lacked in most of them. She checked out one of the closest to her house -experience of lobby was of inducing a striking effect with Chinese lights and furniture copied from European designers imported in a container along with artificial plants and disconcerting rugs, tacky art work imparted the tacky interiors through.

Besides the lack of janitors and not a careful design to unimpressive spaces and sometimes unhygienic too, lacking basic lighting and ventilation seemed to be the norm in many. In some cases, VOC emitted for months, due to lack of air exchanges. The entrance and the facade were gawky. Cafes had property negotiations going on and had taken an ugly impression on her. She had started seeing it as a role-play between four or five people, similar roles repeated.

How easy it is when you know a person you care for, what makes him continue the path and how easy then was to accomplish that. Troubling are people who do not know themselves. They take away so much more from you unknowingly by refusing happiness, its need and acknowledgement.

Abhiyansh wanted to deal with and actually teach her. So he chose his words very carefully.

She was trying the same now with Sumit to sort out the weeds first and could empathise with Abhiyansh. She could not make way. It wouldn't have taken much effort to reach out but he wasn't giving a chance, neither had she, the mind space.

Processing was done on the RAW files, which were much heavier, with only the important ones to identify. The images had a physical feeling, the ones that were retained. This was now a metaphor.

Again, the choice was hers. A leap, for the unseen positive! To change the course of it or to give in to the natural change that was happening and draw far away from him, both find space and move on. The right thing seemed to be to step in each other's shoes and move forward together. But there were too many constraints to overcome to take that path, especially to come back to a normal level from the upheaval of a whirlwind that it was.

CHAPTER 18

Meeting, impromptu

Inertia worked strongly for her. Once set in motion it was difficult to stop. And vice versa.

My lips curl

And the soaring waves engulf me

For, across the cliff I see you smile

Spar in hand

Set on 'the voyage'

Abhiyansh:

I pined for you and pained myself. When you touched, I had walked. It could not reach. I shun you not out of pride; I shun you for I am lifeless. Pain carried away after longing and stopping the hand to connect, life will again move on.

I smile in retaliation of your smile.

Your strength that I have been a part of.

Ria:

Well, there are sad chapters too in the book when the mirage breaks. Or your own belief gets a shocker. I ask for a touch and am denied.

Abhiyansh:

Those bubbles in the baarish....

I would wait for her to feel the same for eternity...only if the bubbles could stay.

I wanted to hold her and tell her what she meant.

The music that brings out the unknown hidden pain from your heart and plays with it.. the pain that follows the chords of the song...chained to them beyond your control. Only with the lyrics playing you are able to breathe again.

Ria:

But how can you taste the most intimate, if you don't delve. Avoid where he would feel fated to loving and then longing and suffering.

Even if the intent was clearly visible in the results, the jury always wanted to know the concept in design. It had to come across. As clearly visible that your intent is right, letting the other person know always helped in a relationship.

The greens outside the pane with the backdrop of sky and if you look, shift your gaze to the broken drops in lines, lots of them, focus through —the drops and the green leaves, the occasional drops still falling, harmonizing with the world.

The lights in perspective along the road, standing out of darkening foliage with the distance, looked serene. Now only if someone could switch off the generator and let the scene sink in perfectly.

As soon as her foot was repaired, a friend took them around for an evening for drinks. And everyone did indulge. Also, there was a one-off play in Gurgaon, in an upcoming theatre: Ekal and the Conman!

The mind in "maybe" mode - everything runs quickly, in flashes, some from the memory. Moments in flashes and the fingers halt a little above the keyboard, the eyes close, breath normalizes and the author gasps.

There was food in front, laughter and easy conversation between the two men on the opposite sides of the table. And some good vibes oozing out from the best man in the whole wide world.

Was it the pink and white of the flowers or was it the subtle beige reflecting off his trousers? All in a daze, or was it like the sky-blue chignon dress, and the colour deepening along with the side helms, of flowing length that she wore.

It was happening in a click, in flashes.

Few promises, business deals. As if set in stone, with a lot of mortar to bind……….flash

"The only thing that looks good on me" playing in the background. Now the extra mortar which could now be brushed. The shape of the sculpture emerging slowly………flash

An ataxic gait….. inside and the theatre lights flashing. And flowers, real flowers….. and the ones set in resins, reachable by hand. Lots of fallen leaves….fibreglass leaves…. and dramatic skies….. and water and reflections. Were they the theatrical lighting or more of flashes or flashes on the forehead or actual reflections?

Ekal: the tortured one! In chains…..The measure of the payment could be money, money in the worldly terms but for Ekal it was the words uttered along with the interaction. And the shared senses heightened by the exchange.

For the muse it's a dream. "Please, let it remain a happy one". The muse says to the artist- lovingly, pleadingly, logically, angrily, happily and then desperately.

And the enforcements of sentiments are first with adoration, then with a right, then with a hope and maybe with a gloom later.

In a prerogative, the muse can decide the format and change the order too.

"It had worked in the past. It doesn't work now", says the artist. He is embarked on his journey where his pursuit pulls him the most and at a bend on the road ahead, he sits, on a chiselled seat and then moves ahead. Whatever is his trip, it is his alone and the deep-down satisfaction or incoherence too his own.

The artist who now takes several muses at a time.

When one muse is treated in a demeaning way or as a tester to another, one muse starts teaching malice to the other. The bond with which each muse is held in a strategy. Different bond agreement with each muse..... so many of them and each positioned without each other's knowing of the rest.

The muse, Ekal having gone through the cycle above addresses when the patience or whatever virtue the muse is held with, runs out.

Ekal wants to upgrade the connotation to a different level and demands the same.

On being addressed, the artist, instead of renewing the bond or connect and sometimes refusing to deal with the complication, tries to man up the ship, wanting to retain the supremacy. He displays a mode the muse is scared of. The muse goes berserk.

For a dignified exit, some protocol must be followed. The muse wants some respect or calmness in the heightened senses. The senses were repressed for too long, now they had to be heightened as a simple logic of nature. "Clean up your act, offer an apology. Show that courage and honour you talk of." Ekal screams in his scare, scare of not being able to look at the furious eyes of the artist.

The hatred wasn't present. It builds up in both. In extremes! One emotion, which reciprocates the worst!

The misleading game had to end somewhere, Ekal always thought and hoped it would end in a better start and not on the next level of misleading.

"In your game of winning another victim, there was a real life of a person involved" he murmured.

Always….. ready to see the human side, empathise and patiently waiting and then demanding sincerity and been thrown back at/ convinced/shown a threat/shown one-man up man ship/shown more anger instead of compassion, a reaction to anger, confrontation and clarity, all the known parameters and applying/bearing the same in reverse too….now the Artist too gives up, gets up from his throne.

How could he? Ekal screamed, but only inside, voice left him even with his persistence. He was shouting, squeezing his mind in disbelief more than the pain that he wasn't given a hearing and still thrashed. By the One truly adored and loved by him.

How could he: just how? Leave one and then take another. The best out of his heart was taken away. Take away or keep the one you have, take another and then leave the first one. How often Ekal had thought, he was the one, he had started with the confidence and the assurance. And rest came and went.

Seasons and people:

The Artist did remember his continued assurance. But he had to get ahead of himself all the time…. The muses knew. Only Ekal didn't. How many times since eternity, that was the signing of the contract, had the Artist tried to let go of Ekal…. He too had pain each time a muse left. But there was one moment and the next and then the next. Those were fleeting moments. Then the moments became longer….. and longer and suddenly shorter. How could he position himself with the muses…..

He had positioned the muses in a circle around him, reaching out. The muses too had their circles around them, their own solar systems, since they were Artists too. He had conned, but how couldn't he? Why couldn't he and he too was suffering? But the throne…. The music… the harder the beats…the cacophony…. Ekal in his chains! And the chains flew…. Chains flew with bangs. Shattered! And the lights dimmed.

Of whom were those chains, the raw, beaten, golden and iron and the black and grey chains? Were those of the Artist or Ekal or so many more…. So many more, one dozen and a half, who entered the stage dimming now and ……. no one took a bow.

The play ended! Stunned or not was the audience…it didn't matter. Neither did the applause. It ended; ended with many facets opened up and no loops closed, or were it the heady mix in her head.

But end it did! So much of it did. The moment of revelation had arrived.

******

So be it! Did it matter! It was pretty relaxing an outing and the friend's flimsy driving back from Sohna road seemed not to mind anyone's presence neither did anyone care.

Carrying the softest of her smiles she came closer to Sumit. He looked relaxed too. She did pay heed to what he would be thinking about. The whole point of achieving this state seemed to be culminating into bonding...flowing into each other's breath. The whole world seemed shapeless. It was just he and she, no words.

Her lips reached out, thoughtlessly, delving in the moment and eyes looking into the stillness in his eyes.

He interluded; said he was not done with his booze ... he needed to go out to the market to bring more. How could that be? It was hurtful. She was in the foreplay on her own without him. It did not feel reasonable.

He pulled away and went towards the door. She wanted to tell him to check the temperature regulator of the son's room-she just couldn't bring herself to utter a word. What seemed to be perfect a setting for the romantic demeanour, it seemed to be fading instantly and unreasonably.

He went out. Now she was thankful for being drunk and not disdaining it. The sleep was overpowering, gratifyingly.

Drug yourself, alter your mind, accentuate certain emotions and douse few and connect to another soul.

The same scenario in complete consciousness, when the harmony of your own self and the others awaken you to bond and melt into each other naturally.

She felt this, just the need to close eyes and the whole being was so calm and in deep sedation of another mental plane. This was ecstasy in itself.

And met with the same consciousness, one of the most beautiful forms of meditation, and gratitude for this beautiful life form manifested in this/these bodies.

He was back in a while wearing a scowl. Sleep was overpowering her. Her bare arms were open and verbally expressed. He did not take her cue or touched." Fun never stops for you; we had a good evening outside". Why do you want the fun to continue, he mumbled in anger.

This shattering and the mix of sleepiness, alcohol, and confusion. The fun outside was relaxation and the culmination was in their intimacy. How could a good evening outside be a pinnacle of it?

May be that is how relationships start falling out. How simple it was to make up and move. Well, if that one hug becomes the point of endless discussion, a reason to begin a fight.....

The belief in clearing the weeds wasn't faltering.

"Now I am distraught- I need to be loved...the times I need to be cared for.

You be fine- let me flow with you. You never seem happy- that immensely troubles. You stopped the flow. Even wrath has to have passion. Or the middle way! Weren't we humans social naturally, yet in co-existence, a difficult species?"

Is this when you need to seek God? When the people you have reciprocally found fulfilment with tell you to seek living beyond them?

Is it then that you start focussing on the lesser, lose your lightness. The shallow becomes easier, the deeper difficult and to "believe" you need a God. Instead of "acknowledging" Him being there. Will you seek heaven in another world? In an afterlife?

It was all here; you could see it if you opened your hands.

We all have to work the same in life. Some of us choose what we work on, what to do ourselves and what to get done.

Few of us work up only our minds and badly so.

When faced with a dilemma, wasn't choosing the right thing the way forward, however difficult it could be. Wasn't loving the only sane way of surviving a real marriage? Inheriting wealth without inheriting the toil associated? If one does, the toil is in some other way for you to balance that wealth with yourself. You give reasons to it. You adjust yourself and the troubles adjust themselves around you. You feel you are not loved. Then you give up expectations or make your way into love.

The emptiness of the soul that hits you sometimes!

Doesn't let you dive in. Would it unfold with the intensity of the search? To fill it up with work, enthusiasm, wellness, people, gratefulness and love. May be with a fierce ambition to top it all with.

Those who were sitting by the seemingly shallow stream, simply witnessing its flow simply seemed so much happier to her and she envied them.

Serenaded by the sun, a touch on the peaks and a reassuring engulf of the entire valley.

The mind could not be kept empty; it needed its own fill. It was complex but if she had quietened herself and moved on, the change and adjustment would not have happened in the right direction.

"I have a selective memory, a swirling pattern too. Slowly and gradually, she remembered only the kindness and tried to keep only the pleasant."

But as people closest to you, become fully sentiment- they can touch you or hurt you the deepest. Who was this you she had been in constant conversation with always. Was it God, Sumit or herself. Or a metaphor!

I have been completely apparent only to YOU

To YOU, I do not think and offer

I get totally aware of myself in your presence.

The consciousness of my own presence

Meeting:

And how incomplete would we have lived if we did not touch in our paths!

"A man waiting for his moment" by Sasha Gusov was on display. In the cold cold January.

On the way to the main hall, displayed was the work of a group of people. Hers too.

"Abhiyansh came back in sight- I saw him. My heart did skip a beat."

She had always got stuck in the eyes, never had noticed the lips before. Now she knew what attraction he held. His affectionate smile and non-surprised behaviour on noticing her was again warm and reassuring just as before.

"She was there right in front of me." Now she was a lovely lady, stunning actually. She has a layer over her now. Now she thinks and talks."

And in a way she would live in me forever, the old unedited version.

We both did not ask for each other's co-ordinates.

"All that you have taught me, I apply. My pictures one day will carry your signature. I always tell my child, my protégé and my viewers about you.

I have you, my camera and the vision you gave me to count on."

He studies her work.

Only I wish, her naivety hadn't changed!

"It was instinctive for me, Ria. Today, I can frame it in words to myself. If I had approached you, you would have craved to meet Aica, she had become a part of me. Will always be!"

Thinking thus and signalling a friend with his renowned laughter ringing in the air and his resolute gait, he walked towards the exit.

At the exit they meet. After all that said that has to be said when you chance to meet an old colleague, exchange news and then it's time to leave. She said goodbye; he said the same. The eyes were simply firm, he scanned for an emotion. These eyes were not confused.

And a handshake…one that was not required!

Him:

Its time to move on. I hoped you would never become worldly. Your spontaneity has given way to 'think and act'. Your honesty of sentiments has given way to "think and speak".

And your pictures, my dear, sweetheart, already carry my signature.

Blissful!

A soul drenched in love, will only end up blessing the beloved.

The laughter to be preserved well,

has to be packaged at source.

And for a beautiful butterfly to fly away.

*****

One might want to experience these with the right people intended. But then existence has it is own way of balancing out. You return to them with some one else if not, with the one intended.

We all have to live our feelings - all of them from the wide plethora, depending on how and with whom? And choose when and where we apply them!

Later, over a late lunch with a friend, a kid with his antics found an amused adult spectator in Ria. He was with his parents in a group of many. Post lunch, over coffee in the outside sitting area, Ria started taking pictures.

The kid followed her to the window from inside. And it was a tiny boy's picture in the big window. Captured herself by the subject, she was capturing a moment.

The connection was his hand on the glass pane looking intently at Ria. The stark illumination was on his palm and the immediate contrast with the darkness around its profile. The next layer of lighting by the sun was on the cheeks bulging out of a face with interested eyes and a naughty smile. With most of the space in the image filled with dark in the deep coloured wooden rectangle of the window, the pale textured sill filled in the bottom of the image with horizontal element.

On both sides of the large window were teal green louvered shutters. The right side taken majorly in the frame and only the edge taken on the left side by the photographer. The foreground was a creeper on the sill, further variegated in illumination by natural sunlight. The teal shutter and the brown wooden frame inside were separated with a white jamb.

The kid in cobalt blue sweatshirt, standing beside faded lime green sofa's back, same as that of leaves outside was Ria's afflatus. All who saw the tasveer in print, the kid's smile met with their own smile.

The friend curating another exhibition did a large sized exhibit, of the little boy with his hand on glass and bought the copyrights.

CHAPTER 19

GOA

Pitter-patter- right after the sudden drift from winter to spring by February end, out of the blue came a waft of droplets from the open window that Ria woke up to. On the first day of March, the fresh greens were sprouting out from the tree trunk in the backyard and the rest looked freshly awashed. In fact, the fresh green from the front window looked too green against the cool chromium grey of the sky. Sumit suggested it would again look ok the next day in the sunshine.

The fumes of steaming coffee mug on the wide top rail against the backdrop of the tree and morning sky were in an upward trail. Then she clicked the same with Sumit's hand reaching out for it in the frame, on her mobile.

No commitment, no expectation now. The motor to change the inertia lay within her perhaps seeking an external key still. Hoping for an acknowledgement.

Life is a journey. Complete it! The milestone had read. The picture of it from a previous vacation was on her mobile phone's wallpaper.

Jump in her heart was missing with he disclosed his Goa plan. It was missing in the journey to Goa as well. Was the complete bliss in togetherness possible again?

Suryansh saw the pool as they reached the resort and ran towards it. Further along, was the sea. A whole wide patch of the view of the sea, as far as you could see between the building frames. He squealed and ran towards the private beach. Ria beamed, stood there for a while and ran towards Suryansh.

A day after, Suryansh started playing with another couple's daughter on the turf. Ria, on her recliner, looked at Sumit. He looked very relaxed. Oh, but they needed to pack and move to the next hotel. Suryansh refused to budge. It was about checkout time. She picked up her shades and they started for the room. The electric current felt strong in her body. Was it coincidental, the proximity and the electric current felt strong in the body and both of their hands reached for each other with feverishness. The pull and the surge were as high as in earlier times. They were rolling over each other.

The sheets were pulled. The eyes met with an intensity matched by the tongues. They were rolling over each other and time stopped. Bodies moved, craving for more.

"There is heaven between us," she exclaims.

"What more do we want" she murmurs

"What more would anyone want," his soft lips say, still in the embrace between the sheets.

You point out the mirror to me. I reluctantly turn my face away from you.

The mirror could have been different, a huge one bordered with a perfectly measured groove all around, a plush white rug on the travertino floor. The gleaming floor could be covered by Turkish carpets under our feet. The space could be larger and surrounded by woods further on. Our wagons outside could be state of the art.

For this, we run our whole lives?

Lo. This image in the mirror means the whole world to me.

How would it alter our heaven? The heaven is right here in us, in our arms. "Together" is where we make our heaven.

Our joy in proximity is celebrated by the clouds!

And it rains when we make love.

****

They shifted to Cidade de Goa. The myriad voids as frames, the courtyards, colours, spaces invited her back to the world of photography. A composition of father and son on the brass jhula in the veranda of a cottage. And the image locked. As they were headed to the suite after a hearty dinner, with vistas growing more ambient for the night photography, shades of colour variations showing up better and the set in shadows, Ria had to stay back and resume with her buddy, the one which was once an extension of her arm. Sumit carried the sleeping child in his arms to the room.

Further on the music from one of the large party places sounded inviting. Ria was smiled at by the Mediterranean looking people on the terrace. A cheerful crowd inside of over a hundred Iranians wore a festive fervour. Dressed in cottons and not at all conservatively, the families and extended families and friends all were in the gusto of dance. The music was lovely and the faces welcoming. Ria placed her camera aside and the enjoyment started seeping in. She almost started feeling like a part of the group.

They cajoled her into joining, she called up Sumit and he came holding the baffled child in his arms. He was very warmly welcomed by a middle-aged bald man, who had earlier welcomed Ria. Soon the two were dancing with them and the half asleep, half bewildered son was in somebody else's lap. A lady explained they were celebrating Iranian New Year, Navroz which happened to be in March. Since this was more liberal a place they had all come to take in the celebration and interspersed more freely.

The night carried on thus and they were made very much a part of the troop on the terrace too. Before the couple excused themselves, their last dance was with the Iranian hosts dancing with them on a Bollywood number. The camera unused, the couple revelled in the experience of how in a friendly way music and cheer could bind us all from anywhere across the globe as the music faded in the distance.

All she remembered from the references, however big or small from the journey was the perspective from the aeroplane window and that she looked like a young belle in the streets of faraway lands.

The world that matters the most is a close sphere around you, the circumference determined by your camera's exposure and understanding of life. Overexposure could give you as much trouble as much as underexposure. Same is with the balanced overlapping of circumferences of our solar systems.

To keep up with the pursuit of the unknown

How about determining the shades by looking into the viewfinder through the lens of your choice?

Lens of hope!

Himanshi found out an employer for Nazma, called her over in the park and took her home leaving her stuff behind. She marked the ad for full-time help in the newspaper and dropped her to the new employer.

Mumtaz saved Ameena. But she didn't want to get deported and Mumtaz found her employment.

Mumtaz's son came over to Abu Dhabi. Her employer from Kerala, a businessman saw to it.

And by virtue of making the deserts green, rain becomes an annual affair in a land two thousand kilometres away from the monsoon.

By virtue of making the desert green, the rainfalls became annual.

"I wore the shades of hope and happiness."

And serendipity followed.

Glossary

1. Jaan - life, loved one
2. Abaya - clothing that is long and covers the body below the neck
3. Kaffeyiah - Arabian headdress, that provides protection from sand and heat
4. Kandura - ankle length robe for men
5. Atar - fragrant oil
6. Oudh - fragrance, pungent yet pleasing
7. Burqa - enveloping outer garment for women
8. Mashrabiya - window screen
9. Jali - grille
10. Kachcha test - driving test, pre final
11. Pakka test - Final driving test
12. Puja - the act of worship
13. Dupatta- stole for women
14. Tasveer - picture
15. Ikkat - fabric made with a decorative technique
16. Shikhara - spire
17. Haveli - mansion
18. Chajjah - balcony
19. Mali - gardener
20. Salwaar - kameez
21. Mitti - gardener
22. Malba - debris
23. Kaajal - black liner used around the eyes
24. Azaan- muslim summon to prayer
25. Souq - market
26. Barjeel - wind tower
27. Arbaab - landlord
28. Asan - yoga body posture
29. Iftaar - after sunset meal during Ramazan

30. Mehnat - hardwork
31. Salat - al- fajr - dawn prayer
32. Adabb - courtesy
33. Anarkali - long flowing frock style garment which creates a flattering flowing silhoutte
34. Mithai - sweet
35. Verandah - porch
36. Shawarma - middle eastern dish
37. Tabla - pair of hand drums from the Indian sub-continent
38. Indra - Hindu diety, associated with sky, lightening, weather
39. Roza - fasts in the month of Ramazan
40. Iftaar - the meal eaten after sunset during Ramazan
41. Laban - buttermilk
42. Kurta - long loose shirt worn in south asia
43. Abra - traditional boat made of wood
44. Mitti - soil
45. Shaikha - female of an Arab ruling family
46. Sheikh - head of an Arab family/ tribe
47. Imam - one who leads prayers in a mosque
48. Tumhari - yours
49. Amma - mother
50. Eidi - gift for children on Eid by elders
51. Chor gali - backstreet
52. Bhagwan - God
53. Baarish- rain
54. Jhumka – ear adornment
55. Zakat - charity
56. Bhai - brother
57. Roti - wheat bread
58. Sheesha - oriental tobacco apparatus
59. Khad - fertilizer
60. Juicewalla - juice vendor

61. Jhula - swing

62. Fattura – fine

63. Sawab ki kamai – hard earned money

251

Disclaimer: This book is a work of fiction. Names, characters, places and incidents are products of the author's imagination or are used fictitiously. Any resemblance to actual events or locales or persons, living or dead, is entirely coincidental.

About The Author

Shikha S is based in Gurgaon, India. "Through the shades" is her first literary work on a professional scale. Words as she sees, are a mode of not only expression, but also as a tool to achieve higher pursuits. She believes that the dictionary revolves around words like joy, serendipity, happiness and most importantly, the shades we wear on our soul. And soul being an index of the mind, just as the eyes are...

She is a farmer's daughter. Architecture, travel, music, art and culture she feels and believes, are synonymous to our living. And they bind us all. All of us, without the boundaries, demarcated or created.

She has been an editor throughout her school and college years. At present she enjoys being an architect, an artist and a photographer.